CW01429938

LISTEN, IT'S WEDNESDAY

CHRIS VALE

LISTEN, IT'S WEDNESDAY

The Book Guild Ltd

First published in Great Britain in 2017 by
The Book Guild Ltd
9 Priory Business Park
Wistow Road, Kibworth
Leicestershire, LE8 0RX
Freephone: 0800 999 2982
www.bookguild.co.uk
Email: info@bookguild.co.uk
Twitter: @bookguild

Copyright © 2017 Chris Vale

The right of Chris Vale to be identified as the author of this
work has been asserted by her in accordance with the
Copyright, Design and Patents Act 1988.

All rights reserved. No part of this publication may be
reproduced, transmitted, or stored in a retrieval system, in any form or by any means,
without permission in writing from the publisher, nor be otherwise circulated in
any form of binding or cover other than that in which it is published and without
a similar condition being imposed on the subsequent purchaser.

This work is entirely fictitious and bears no resemblance to any persons living or dead.

Typeset in Minion Pro

Printed and bound in Great Britain by 4edge Limited

ISBN 978 1912083 237

British Library Cataloguing in Publication Data.
A catalogue record for this book is available from the British Library.

Printed on FSC accredited paper

AUTHOR OF

Brassy Women,
The Brass Bass Legacy
The Rhythm Cats

The action takes place in the sixties, when women brass players were few and there was no talk of 'alternative' lifestyles.

All the characters are imaginary.

No resemblance to any living person is intended.

1

Quite calm now that she had made the decision, Ruth weighed up the possibilities. She had several options, and whichever one she chose she was going to help matters along with the rest of the whisky. In the kitchen, she opened the high cupboard and found a glass. As she placed it on the table, the carving knife glinted back at her invitingly. Should she cut her wrists? It would be messy, but she could do it in the bath. The blood would run nicely away down the plughole, so that all the landlord would stumble upon when some time in the future he called to claim the unpaid rent, would be a pale corpse and a discreet red line leading to the drain.

She went into the bathroom where the bath gleamed white and unsullied like a page which had not yet been written on. Should she climb into it? No. The blood might get all over her clothes, creating a horrifying sight for the unfortunate landlord. So she folded herself face down over the side, ready to slump into it as unconsciousness overtook her. She held out her left wrist. The blue tracery of veins was plain to see. She placed the edge of the knife against it and told herself to do it. Now!

But she could not bear to bring the blade down hard enough to cut the vein. She straightened up and looked for inspiration around her. Could she strangle herself with a towel tied to the back of the door? She had heard of people who had succeeded in hanging themselves that way, but she could not work out how to go about it. That little hook on the back of this door was hardly strong enough to take a bath robe. A human form, if attached, would surely end up in an ignominious heap on the floor.

She opened the door of the little cabinet that hung on the wall at eye level. Talc, foot cream, body lotion, iodine were ranged on the lower shelf. On the higher one between the eye lotion and the sticking plasters were the pills.

Sarah's sleeping pills. The bottle was more than half full of the pills which Sarah would not now need. She took them gratefully and put them on the coffee table in the lounge, adding the bottle of whisky and a glass.

All that was lacking now was some music. Something that would last long enough to see her out. She opened the record cabinet and ran her eyes over the spines of the LP's. Haydn's Trumpet Concerto? No, it was too lively. Beethoven? Too noisy. Her LP of Frank Sinatra singing sad songs? Tempting, but it might make her too busy crying to keep swallowing. All the jazz numbers were on 78s. Three minutes a side would not do. She wished she had a tape of Lucy's band. She would have been able to fade out to the sounds of *Eventide*.

In the end she decided that Tchaikovsky's Pathetique Symphony would strike the right chord. Her cornet and her trumpet sat side by side in their respective cases on top of the gramophone. She had to move them onto the floor in order to open the lid and gain access to the turntable. She felt a little pang of regret. Did they have trumpets in Heaven? Of course they did. They had golden ones, no less, and sackbuts and dulcimers and harps.

But then, would she get there? God had been an ever-present help in trouble in her childhood. That was before she had turned her back on him. A bit late now to say she had changed her mind.

She was not his sort any more. She had rejected him and now it was too late. She belonged to nobody. The best she could hope for was total oblivion. That was what she craved.

The turntable turned, the arm went down and bassoons clawed their way up through the first sad bars of the desolate symphony, aided and abetted by the double bass. She thumped up all the cushions, removed her shoes and stretched out on the sofa. First of all she poured a generous tot of neat whisky. Then one by one she started on the pills. She took her time. There was no hurry. Nobody would interrupt her. Nobody was going to be coming home.

Lucy and Eileen packed their shopping into the boot of the Mini and headed for the main road.

"Are you in a hurry to get back?" Lucy asked.

"Not more than usual. Did you want to call in somewhere?"

"Do you mind if we drop by at Ruth Anderton's place? She knows more than anybody about band music."

"She'll never be in at this time, surely. You can raise the subject on Wednesday. She'll be at t' practice."

"It's not far out of our way. I'd just like to get her recommendation for new pieces; ask if she knows a good place to go to for a set of band parts. There's too many other people wanting my attention at t'practice."

That was the best explanation Lucy could think of to justify the compulsion she felt to go and see Ruth.

"What does she do for a living anyway?" Eileen wanted to know. She was not keen to descend on her unannounced.

"Haven't a clue."

They turned into quite a nice residential estate just out of Chorley town centre and stopped the Mini in the road outside Ruth's house. Lucy climbed out but Eileen insisted on staying put.

"She'll not be there. Take my word for it."

But she was there.

Lucy's finger had hardly left the bell when the door was snatched open and there stood Ruth, alight with hope. At the sight of Lucy, her face crumpled like a ball of paper. Two tears tried to ooze their way out from behind the tightly-clenched lids. Lucy stood there appalled. Then she gathered her wits and ushered Ruth inside to the privacy of her lounge, where Tchaikovsky at his most fraught was filling the air with twenty-four carat anguish. Lucy sat Ruth down on the settee.

"What's happened?" she asked. "Can I do anything?"

"No." The voice was muffled. Ruth had picked up a cushion and was holding it over her face, blotting everything out. "Go away."

"You may as well know that I'm not going away and leaving you like this. Tell me what's wrong."

"Have a drink, then," Ruth offered, throwing the cushion down and wiping her puffy eyes with the back of her hand. "Pour one for me at the same time."

Lucy looked at her sharply. She would have said that a few drinks had already gone that way.

"I don't want a drink."

"I do. It's over there."

Ruth waved a hand at the sideboard, where she had placed the bottle on her way to answer the door. The water and pills she had hastily consigned to the kitchen. So Lucy found a glass and poured a middle-sized tot. She then decided it might be wise in the circumstances to add some water. It was just as well that she did, because when she went into the kitchen to turn on the tap she found a used glass with some sediment in the bottom. There was a half-empty pill bottle on the draining board.

She picked it up, read the label and tipped the whisky down the sink. When she returned to the lounge, Ruth had slumped forwards with her head in the cushion and nearly rolled off the settee when Lucy shook her shoulder.

"How many did you take, Ruth?"

"I dunno. Didn't count."

"Where's your telephone?"

"Nowhere. Leave me alone. Why did you come?"

Lucy switched off the gramophone, found the phone and rang for an ambulance. Then she ran outside to fetch Eileen.

"What's up, Lucy? You look terrible."

"I look terrible? Wait till you see Ruth."

The object of their concern was sprawled on the sofa with her mouth open. Her eyes and nose had been running. Lucy fished out a tissue from her handbag and mopped them, as she would the face of a small child. Ruth was trying with all her might to lose consciousness, but had not yet succeeded. Eileen shook her rather gingerly, causing Ruth to sit up and wave her away. But her voice was thick when she spoke.

"I'm all right," she insisted. "Go away. Why did you come? I didn't ask you to come. Where's my hanky?"

"You're not all right," Lucy told her firmly, rifling Eileen's handbag for another tissue, "and you know it. How many have you taken?"

"How the hell do I know?" Ruth started to cry. "Leave me alone. You shouldn't be here. I want to die."

"You're not going to die, Ruth."

"I want to die. Leave me alone."

"We need you. We need you in the band. We are not going to let you die. Understand that much."

Lucy and Eileen looked at one another uncertainly.

"We're not going to let you die," Eileen felt she ought to add in support of Lucy.

"I feel sick," announced Ruth.

They each grabbed an arm.

"Where's your toilet?"

"I don't feel that sick."

"You will, if I have anything to do with it."

The ambulance soon arrived. The paramedics took control of

the situation with well-practised efficiency and whisked Ruth away, leaving a rather shaky pair of middle-aged ladies to contact her next of kin.

Next of kin?

"Try the desk," said Elaine.

They riffled rather guiltily through her desk and phone book until Lucy came across a list of phone numbers. The top one just had the name 'Ricky' with a local number. She had no idea of the person's age or even sex, when she dialled the number. It was answered by the rather plangent voice of a young male, who reacted with dismay.

"Oh my God no! Where's Sarah, then?"

"I don't know. I haven't asked. There's no sign of anyone else here."

"What a disaster! I'll get over to see her as soon as I can. I can't stop. I'm at work and there's a customer waiting."

"Bless you, Ricky. Tell her Lucy will call round and see her tomorrow."

Ruth was unconscious by the time she was pumped out. They left her on one of the beds at the end of a ward to recover, ready to turn her out again into the cruel world. The mists floated before her eyes. She was aware of the clack of feet on linoleum. Then somebody took her hand. She made out the shape of a head. It was all right. Sarah was there.

But when she opened her eyes properly the mists cleared and there was no mistaking Ricky's large kind eyes and his bony face as he peered anxiously towards her. A feeling of desolation swept over her and she began to cry again, quietly.

"Take it easy," said Ricky. "When you're ready I'll drive you home."

That was all he could think of to say. He knew how she felt. He knew that nothing he could say would make it any better. He could only be there so that she was not alone.

6

2

Lucy spent the weekend telephoning band members to put them in the picture and make sure they treated Ruth right when next she came to their practice night. The would-be suicide was the band's top cornet and they could not afford to lose her. It was her knowledge of music which had saved her life. Or would Lucy have found another reason to call round when she did? Dropping in on people unannounced was not something she was prone to.

So on Tuesday she telephoned before making another visit. Band practices were on Wednesday evenings. Lucy wanted to make sure that Ruth was not only fit to attend, but willing to do so. She did not have any piano pupils until the afternoon, which made mid-morning the best time. The person who opened the door to her this time was pale and subdued, but mercifully recovered.

"Cup of tea?"

"I'd love one."

They talked about music. They both had a wide-ranging knowledge of both the piano and the orchestral repertoire. When offered some background music on the record-player, Lucy chose Mozart's *Eine Kleine Nachtmusik,* as being about the most cheerful she could think of, off-hand. Ruth asked where Lucy had studied and with whom, but every time Lucy tried to probe Ruth's background in return, she was stalled by another question.

No matter. The important point to get across was that, having dragged her back from the brink, she would expect Ruth to attend the practice as normal on the following Wednesday.

So when Wednesday evening crawled into view, Ruth threw her cornet onto the back seat of her Hillman Minx as usual and drove to Rivington Church Hall. The familiar activity raised her spirits as she made for the double doors of the entrance. Noises inside were amplified by the bare-walled interior. She could hear Alice and Gladys, the first and second trombones, contradicting one another while their sister Florence tried to drown them out with her bass trombone warm-up exercises.

Gladys bickered with everybody. She was the band complainer, the second sister of four, the second trombonist of three, who were all now in their forties.

As the rest of the band arrived the general hubbub increased, with the clack of shoes on the wooden floor, the moving of chairs, the clink of instruments and of course the exchange of greetings, the passing on of news, the various muttered comments.

Ruth walked in quietly. She went straight to her chair and set up her music stand, meeting nobody's eye. There was a brief moment of silence, before conversations were resumed and instruments were blown into to warm them up and reassuring normality returned. Lucy gazed around the room and noted with satisfaction that Ruth had arrived. She looked lacklustre but at least, Lucy told herself, she was there, which was more than could be said for Annette, who played the trumpet and was Ruth's second in command. Perhaps she should not have asked her to pick up a new bass player called Sally. Annette drove her husband's capacious Jaguar, which was why Lucy had singled her out as the person most suitable to transport somebody with an instrument the size of a double B flat bass. She had dictated the directions for finding Sally's flat over the phone. Had Annette forgotten this new duty? Had she mislaid Sally's address? Or had she got lost looking for the featureless flat? No matter, the band would just have to soldier on without them for now. "*Regimental Selection,*" she announced.

Groaning a little, for it was not their favourite piece, the women of Lucy Brindle's Ladies Brass Band, or such of them as were present, put up the music on their stands and sprang into action as the baton fell. They were tramping through the final repeat of *None But The Brave* when the door opened and in swept Annette with a grim face and a suppressed rage that set the air about her quivering for a distance of several feet. She plonked herself onto the seat next to Ruth, greeting all smiles with a frozen stare and uttered a distinct four-letter word when she trapped her finger in a hurried attempt to open her expensive but complex music stand.

"Leave that for now," Lucy advised her, after the dying notes had failed to cover the expletive. "Read over Ruth's music."

"I'd rather have my own, if you don't mind," snapped Annette.

Then she heard the communal sharp intake of breath and remembered the phone call which Lucy had made at the weekend. "Treat her with kid gloves," had been the general drift. Well, she had certainly knocked that one on the head. Futile to walk out and come in again, only with a different opening line. She wished herself on the other side of the earth, preferably somewhere warm and sunny with a swimming pool and a bronzed and muscular young...

"What's the matter?" Ruth spoke at last. "Don't you fancy me any more?"

Somebody giggled. The tension was broken and they resumed their journey through the succession of well-known marches, interrupted only by the occasional call for a halt.

Annette had had a bad day.

Just before leaving she had had a big row with Harold over

the housekeeping money. Then as she brushed her flowing locks as a prelude to going out, she had found a grey hair, the shock of which had caused her to forget to take with her the written directions to the bass-player's house. She had indeed become lost, as Lucy feared. But when she did eventually find the place, Sally could not leave because her husband had failed to come home on time, and until he did there was no one to babysit her two small children. The whole exercise had been a waste of time.

Now she had made this gaffe. The band broke up for a chat and a knit or a smoke or a trip to the toilet, Annette decided to try cleaning out the valve casings. If she could loosen up first valve, that at least would dispose of one minor irritant. She must also somehow make amends to Ruth.

"What do you do when the valve's sticking?" she asked her colleague conversationally, in what she hoped was a friendly tone of voice. "I've tried everything from bicycle oil to washing-up liquid."

Getting no reply she looked up from her valve casings and saw that Ruth was staring into the middle distance, seeing nothing and hearing nothing, immersed in her own private grief.

"I'm sorry about Sarah," Annette blurted out impulsively. "Come for a drink at the Black Horse afterwards."

"Thanks," said Ruth.

The invitation took her quite by surprise. Kindness was harder to cope with than mockery. With a face that was as stiff as cardboard, she placed her cornet under her chair, away from careless feet, and strode outside for a good howl in the privacy of darkness. Lucy saw her go and was in two minds whether to follow. Was she still contemplating suicide? She raised her eyebrows at Annette, who shook her head and returned to her valves. A bonus from the situation was that all three valves were working splendidly by the time Ruth reappeared, red-eyed and reeking of cigarette.

Lucy rapped on her music stand to call her players back to business. The knitters rolled up their wool and resumed their instruments.

"Get out *Eventide*," she ordered.

"Again?" moaned Gladys.

Again. For now." Lucy told her. "The church has offered us the use of this hall for a bring and buy sale," she added, glaring at Rebecca, who was still reading a comic. "So that we can raise some funds and buy some more music. It's something we badly need, but of course it costs money. So I hope you'll all give every support to this sale."

They all made supportive noises.

"In the meantime we'll play *Eventide*. It's useful for improving tone and breathing. Take a deep breath before you start. Everybody ready?"

She brought the baton down with as slow a tempo as she thought she could get away with and the room was filled with the strong and mellow sound of brass blending in harmony.

Afterwards Ruth packed away her cornet in its case.

"That was thirsty work," she heard Annette say as she clicked it shut. "I'm really looking forward to that drink. Are you?"

"Yes. Now you mention it."

She was. She followed Annette outside, calling the usual goodbyes. She climbed into her own comparatively modest Hillman Minx and directed it to the car park of the Black Horse, where Annette was already waiting at the wheel of Harold's Jaguar. Seeing Ruth arrive she climbed out gracefully, knees together, head inclined. She had a natural and unaffected elegance.

"It won't do you any good to be seen with me," Ruth felt she ought to warn her, after scrambling out of her small doorway with all the grace of a sack of coal.

"It doesn't do me any good to be seen with anybody. I

couldn't help an old cripple across the road without somebody telling Harold they've seen me with another man."

"You'll just have to stop helping cripples then, won't you."

Annette gave her a friendly push.

The Black Horse stood on a crossroads and picked up custom from the traffic between Manchester and the coast. It was well situated at maximum thirst point from both directions. Ruth put her shoulder against the door and they entered a lounge bar full of sales representatives telling each other the latest questionable joke about sales representatives. Women were few. Several eyes lit up when they saw Annette.

Ruth bought the drinks, because she realised that if Annette went to the bar, that would be the end of her own evening.

"Well," she said as she placed two glasses on the table and sat down, "here's to you, me and Regimental Selection. Want some nuts?"

Annette laughed.

"No thanks."

Her companion may have been a bit of a weirdo, but she did have a sense of humour.

Ruth settled herself into the corner chair. She stretched out her legs comfortably. With her dark curly hair and her slim figure she was not unattractive, but her movements tended to be unfeminine.

"Harold doesn't mind you going for a drink without him?" she began.

"I hope not. He's always going for one without me. It's a way of life to him."

"Business?"

"Mostly. Or so he would have me believe. Anyway I've left him babysitting this evening. Let him get to know his kids." She shook back her burnished locks. "No, to be fair, he does take us out sometimes, if there isn't a rugby match on. We took the kids for a drive up to the moors the other day when it was fine. We turned them out of the car and they were off like a pack of wild dogs, but Harold and I could only take a little walk together. He's terribly unfit. Gets breathless if he has to exert himself."

"Too many business lunches?"

"He's under the doctor, anyway. Meanwhile he has to be careful. I have to keep the children amused myself most of the time."

"They're the centre of your life, aren't they. Your children."

"They have to be. They have to be the centre of somebody's life. There's no other way. They need me, poor little beggars."

Ruth stared at the life that was going on around her. The barman pouring drinks, exchanging jokes with customers. The trio playing dominoes in a corner. They would go home to wives and children, sooner if not later, those men whose paths were briefly crossing as they went about their recreation, before returning to their families. Annette would return to hers. She felt desperately empty inside.

"So make the most of your freedom," Annette continued, seeing how desolate she looked, "before it happens to you."

But that was not the right thing to say either.

"It won't happen to me, Annette."

They each sat thinking her own thoughts for a minute. Two business men in their forties turned their backs on the bar and stared across the room speculatively.

"Are you still playing with the Stonemasons?" inquired Annette, choosing a subject, which she hoped would turn Ruth's mind in a more positive direction.

"Yes I am. We've been asked to do regular Saturdays at the Granary. Fridays too, if the demand is there."

"Is it a good place to be? Or is it the back of beyond?"

"I think we hit lucky. The Granary's becoming more popular all the time. People are beginning to beat a path to its doors."

13

"I like that name… the Stonemasons. It has a good ring to it. Was it your idea?"

"Heavens, no! They were the Stonemasons already when I answered their advertisement for players. It was just Donny Mason and Ron Stone originally. They happened to have the right kind of names…"

"… To put together for the name of a group, you mean. Good job they weren't called Donny Dick and Ron Head."

Ruth smothered a laugh.

"I wouldn't have expected that kind of joke from you!"

"I've got three sons." Annette pointed out.

"Ah! Say no more," nodded Ruth. "Anyway," she continued, "Donny and Ron really wanted a young chap like themselves. They're both younger than me."

"Does that bother you?"

"Not particularly. I think sometimes it bothers Donny. He has to be boss. He can't put one over on me like he can the others. Can't get me to bed either, of course. But that's a good thing. I suppose a normal girl could easily break them all up."

"Couldn't they get a chap?"

"I'm sure they could have. They got Ricky Balfour for bass guitar. He's about my age. He answered the same ad as I did. But when Donny discovered I could do vocals and rhythm guitar and could add a bit of colour with the trumpet too, maybe he thought I was worth a try."

"Who wouldn't?"

Ruth held up her glass to the light, swilled the brandy round a little, sniffed its bouquet and sipped, pretending to be a connoisseur.

"I set the chords for everybody and can write lyrics and melodies," she continued, "I planned to make myself indispensable."

"And yet you were ready to throw all that away."

"Yes. I nearly threw it all away. Just like that. You think

14

something is more important to you than anything else and then suddenly... it's dust and ashes."

Her voice fell away.

There was a pause. Annette asked herself whether it would be wise to say that it was Sarah that was dust and ashes as far as she could see. No, it was not wise.

"Anyway," Ruth was speaking again. "maybe it's as well that Lucy came along when she did. We've had an invitation to take part in a Rock and Roll Festival in Manchester and the TV cameras will be there. I should hate to have missed that."

"You know sometimes I envy you."

Ruth's jaw dropped. She looked searchingly into Annette's green eyes. But there was no mockery there.

"But, Annette, you've got everything. I mean everything. I mean is there one single thing you haven't got? Leaving out the TV cameras, of course, which I'm sure could be achieved any time you want to smile at the right person."

Annette dropped her gaze and fingered the stem of her glass, but before she could frame a reply two smartly-suited business men appeared at the spare chairs of their table.

"Is anyone sitting here?" asked one of the men.

"Not yet," Ruth told them uninvitingly.

"Could you take pity on two hard-working business men at the end of a long day?" he asked.

"What do you think, Ruth?" said Annette. "Could we take pity on two hard-working business men at the end of a long day?"

"It depends," replied Ruth, "on what they mean by pity."

The first man, who was obviously the driving force behind the move, sat himself down by Annette.

"We hoped you wouldn't mind if we joined you. I'm Gerald. This is Peter."

Peter sat down too. He had an unassuming air and decent, regular features, but Ruth regarded them both coldly, while

15

Annette gave them her Mona Lisa smile to keep them at bay without frightening them off.

"I said to Peter... we can't leave those two very attractive young ladies on their own, didn't I, Peter. Can I buy you a drink?"

"No thanks," they chorused.

"We've just clinched a deal in Manchester, haven't we, Peter? We thought we'd drop off here for a meal. Highly recommended. Friend of mine said it was the best value this side of Liverpool."

"Was that Charlie White?" Peter spoke at last.

"No. Percy Jenkins."

"Oh him!"

"Yes, him. Pathetic Perce. Should have known better."

"My steak was pure escallop de welly."

"Yes and what about the prawn cocktail? Parsley and Mayo."

"You ought to complain," Annette managed to slip in.

"Yes," agreed Ruth. She did not wish to spend the rest of her evening listening to the kind of discourse she would have switched off had there been a switch. "I'd go and complain if I were you."

"My dear, I already have," countered Gerald, giving her a narrow-eyed stare. "They sent us in here for a free drink. That's our compensation. And so are you, both of you."

Peter, trying not to cringe for his friend, felt it was time to establish the measure of availability of their companions.

"So what brings you two young ladies out this evening? Husbands away? Or are you taking a break from the square-eyed monster?"

"We're trumpet-players," Annette told him mischievously, watching his eyes. "We've been playing trumpets all evening. Now we've come for a drink. Because it makes you thirsty, playing the trumpet."

The two men looked at one another uncertainly. Then they roared with laughter. Ruth felt herself go tense.

"I say, Peter, do you remember that film? What's it called?"

"Yes, I know the one you mean, Gerald, where she plays… "

"There's this fantastic old car. Veteran – no – vintage. Kenneth Moore. It starred Kenneth Moore."

"She stands up in this nightclub…"

"Yes and everybody thinks she's going to be bloody awful, excuse my French…"

"It's called *Genevieve*," interrupted Ruth, feeling her smile turn into a snarl.

"You've seen it."

"Everybody's seen it."

"Do you really play the trumpet?" ventured Peter, feeling something was wrong.

"She's very good, actually," Annette felt obliged to tell him.

"You're not bad yourself," Ruth had to say.

"It's nice of you to say so."

"On your good days, of course."

"I didn't realise this was a mutual admiration society." It was Gerald's turn to snarl.

Ruth drained her glass and rose.

"I've got to go now, folks," she told them and she made her way to the Ladies. If she stayed here, there would be some nasty things said. She knew that from experience. If this was what Annette wanted, let her sort it out for herself. She would slip out the back way.

She found herself thinking of how she and Sarah would have handled the situation. She recalled the perfect understanding with which they would have dealt quite painlessly with Gerald. The ache and the loneliness welled up inside her like a symphony which had never quite been silent but was just now building to a powerful tutto complete with cymbals, thundering timps and a full brass section blowing double forte.

All that was suddenly dispelled by the swish of the cloakroom door and a click of heels.

"Ruth! Are you there?"

"If you mean me, yes."

"Are you all right?" Annette had half feared to find her with slashed wrists bleeding into a bowl. "You're not running out on me?"

"Of course I'm running out on you," came Ruth's voice.

"But there's two of them."

Ruth emerged from her cubicle and washed her hands, letting the water flow over wrists and palms even as she renounced any part in the situation.

"I'm sure you can handle it."

"I'm sorry, Ruth. I wanted to cheer you up."

"You did cheer me up." It was not a total lie. She had felt better for a while. "I'm grateful."

"I didn't ask them to join us. It's not my fault."

"It's your fault for looking like you do," Ruth told her, pulling out a length of roller towel and drying her hands.

"What do you want me to do? Black out some teeth and shave my head?" protested Annette.

"You'd still knock 'em cold," Ruth insisted. "Come on. We can both make a getaway through the back door."

So that is what they did.

3

The room was full of ladders and ropes and men clambering around scaffolding. Wires snaked all over the floor. Flexes hung in festoons. Silent cameras on oiled wheels glided around like the ghosts of Martians. Boom microphones swung about at head level. A woman with a clip-board and horn rimmed spectacles was organising people and dispatching them to make-up rooms. Her hair was cut short and square with a fringe and the sides curving chinward. Men called to one another; swore at one another; asked where the hell was the Grips? And who was responsible for this cock-up?

Impossible to believe that one of the week's most popular TV programmes was shortly to go on air, and not a rope or a ladder would be in sight. Or so they hoped. To one side of the set, a hand-picked section of teenage audience, predominantly female, was being drilled to scream on cue. By the entrance door the first rock and roll group was lined up biting its nails, while the others were being given their order of appearance.

Ruth and her three colleagues had managed to get a good look at the equipment that had been set up in readiness. There were so many gadgets and so much machinery that a person could be forgiven for thinking that you could just turn a switch and let the contraptions get on with it, leaving out people altogether.

A heavily made-up man with a smile like an ostrich began to utter enthusiasms into a camera lens and they knew they were on air. The first group struck up and the audience gyrated, screaming in all the right places. With music that consisted of the long-term repetition of two bars, the visual effect was important. This was picnic time for the camera men. They were ten times as inventive as the performers, but nobody payed much attention to their skills. All the glory was reserved for a clutch of pasty-faced youths in natty clothes and careful hairdos whose singing would not have won the prize at the local pub talent contest.

That was immaterial, though, since they could hardly be heard above a noise that was more appropriate to the engine room of an ocean liner than to a hall converted for the occasion into a TV studio.

There could be no doubt that this was overwhelmingly a boys' occasion. Most members of the female sex were confined to a corner where they were expected to scream their little heads off whatever the music. Ruth was relieved to find that she was not quite the only girl allowed into the performers' arena. There was a vocals trio of young ladies, shivering in scanty dress and asking one another if their eye liner was smudged. That seemed to be the only other representation of the fair sex that Ruth could detect, until she spotted a female drummer, almost hidden by the three lads in her group. The four of them were standing in the area reserved for hopeful fill-ins, who would not be shown on TV, but who might be given a short set afterwards for the benefit of those who wanted to stay on and make a day of it. They had to wait on one side until the cameras had gone before taking a turn.

Ruth found a radiator to sit on and Ricky came to join her. He preferred her company to that of the others, whose hard drinking and womanising was not to his taste. Still concerned for her well-being, he had put an arm around her shoulders. They both knew it did not mean anything, except that they understood one another. One day they would realise that this could be a better basis for a relationship than sexual desire, which comes and goes like the wind, leaving a trail of havoc in its wake.

But that day had not yet arrived.

For the present, Ruth was studying the female drummer. Her eyes continued to be drawn in that direction against her better judgment. The object of her gaze was small in stature. Her sticks never left her hand. Even as she had to stand and watch the others perform, she rapped them against her palm or her thigh, obviously itching to use them for real. She had short fair hair and eyes the colour of forget-me-nots.

Dangerous.

Ruth's contemplations were soon interrupted by Donny and Ron who pushed up, gesticulating to Ricky and herself to get a move on. It was to be their turn in a matter of seconds. They hastened to their stations. The signal was given. Ruth gave a short intro on the keyboard, then Donny struck the percussive flurry that let everybody know in no uncertain terms that the Stonemasons had arrived. Ron yelled the vocals into the highly-sensitive microphone, before picking out a few bits of tune on his guitar, while Donny and Ricky kept the rhythm going on drums and bass. This gave Ruth time to leave the keyboard and pick up her trumpet.

What she played required a fraction of the technique she would need for a good solo with the band. It was wild, undisciplined stuff which spoke to the young audience at gut level. It told of the pain of the human heart; the wonder of kindness; the joy of achievement, and the pity of lost love. Its soaring, plunging lines and stabbing, repeated notes, its wails and its vertiginous expeditions to the high register woke the world, as it had already woken the Granary, to the Anderton trumpet experience. The clamour that followed was genuine.

Quite a few noses were out of joint by the time the sound technicians were cutting the applause. Even Donny looked a bit sour. But he was canny enough to know when he was on to a good thing. So her kissed her afterwards on the forehead and thumped her lightly in the side and called her Satchmo and she was not displeased.

A bulky man in a camel-hair overcoat button-holed Donny and led him away. Ron and Ricky occupied themselves removing such musical equipment as was theirs. Ruth rescued her trumpet to make sure it did not get picked up by mistake, since its case was fairly anonymous. Then she shouldered Ricky's bass guitar by its strap for the same reason.

It seemed a bit tame simply to walk out after the excitement. Should she find Donny and see what the man in the overcoat wanted with him? She scanned the room. Everyone was on the move. On the other side of about a hundred busy people, the female drummer was looking straight in her direction. Their eyes met.

Ruth hesitated. Then forgetting to be wise, she began to push through the hundred busy people who were not going her way. However she was saved from her folly by the woman with the horn rims, who waylaid her well before she was half way across the room.

"I thought you were fantastic!" she gushed, clutching at her sleeve with nicotined fingers.

"Thanks."

It was a worthy compliment, coming from someone who was part of the set-up.

"Fantastic! I've done a lot of these jobs and it's nice to see a bit of talent in the girls, for a change."

She held a cigarette to her shoulder in an affected kind of way. Her eyes ogled a bit.

"Oh really?" hedged Ruth. She was thinking: 'Do I ever look like that?'

"Why don't you come and play at the club some time?"

"Club?"

"The Sapphire. In Manchester? You know it?"

"I think I've heard of it," lied Ruth.

"I can fix it for you, any time. It's all-women, of course."

"Oh!"

Ruth heard the alarm bells at the same time as she saw the green light. It was not a state of affairs to give rise to a quick response.

"Drop in and see for yourself anytime you're passing. Just mention my name." she handed Ruth a card. "They've got a nice little group in there. All girls," she added, in case Ruth had missed the point, "and they'd be happy to have someone of your quality sit in with them."

She left. Ruth looked at the card. Muriel Helpman. Never heard of her. Looking up, she saw Ricky approaching with his empty case, in quest of its contents. He raised a significant eyebrow. She quickly put the card into her handbag.

The girl with the blue eyes had made it to the stage with her group and was happily adjusting her drummer's seat while a couple of incredibly thin and callow youths twiddled guitar pegs and plugged in connections.

Ruth put a detaining hand on Ricky's arm.

"Let's see what they're like."

He clicked his tongue disapprovingly. He knew the workings of her mind. But he reunited the bass guitar with its case while he stood and watched with her. As expected, the newcomers lacked beef in their performance and their music was a pale imitation of one of the top groups. But the drummer threw herself into her role with all guns firing. She had skill, she had commitment. She was good, in fact.

"Come on," urged Ricky, as a spattering of light applause greeted the end of the number. "We don't want the minibus to leave us behind."

"Can you read their name?" Ruth asked him as the tide of people carried them through the door.

"Looks like *RaggleTaggle* from here." He pulled a face. "Silly name."

They wove a way through a maze of assorted vehicles until they found their own and clambered aboard.

"The sillier the better in this line of business," Ruth observed as they stacked the larger instruments above their heads and the smaller ones under the seats.

He smiled to himself, but said nothing.

The following Wednesday Ruth made a point of turning up promptly for the weekly band practice. She wanted to catch Lucy before there were too many people about. As it happened Lucy was just ransacking the music folders for soprano cornet parts when she found Ruth at her elbow. A new girl had arrived, who played soprano cornet and it was a good idea to get all her music out now rather than hold up the practice looking for the soprano part in each piece as it came along.

Ruth held out a large fat envelope.

"Present for the band. With my thanks," she said, and retired to her chair with an awkward stride that betrayed her shyness. There was no need to say what she was thanking Lucy for. Neither of them had mentioned her attempted suicide since it happened. Neither of them wanted to. This was Ruth's way of saying 'thank you'.

Lucy pulled out the contents and discovered a full set of parts for a piece which announced itself as *Black Rock Bay*. It featured a solo bass trombone. Ruth knew that the trombone section was the strongest in the band and, unusually, Florence on the bass was the best, or at least the most extrovert, of the three. In most of what they played her talents were under-used. Here was a chance for her to shine.

Lucy took it straight across to Florence and silently put

24

the solo part on her music stand. Then she started placing the relevant parts on the rest of the stands. She was half way across the room when she heard the exclamation of delight.

"What's this?" boomed Florrie, flexing her slide and squinting at the page. "Recognition at last?"

"It's a present from Ruth," Lucy told her without, mercifully, making a speech about it. "Seats, everybody. Let's give it a run-through."

It had a well set-out conductor's part, which was a luxury for Lucy, since she often had to read from a spare solo cornet part and guess who was doing what from the lines cued-in in small notes. She was amazed to see that there was a good part for soprano cornet. Was Ruth psychic? Probably not, because it opened with percussion.

"It should be stick on cymbal," she told them. "I'll have to rap it out with the baton for now."

So she tapped out the opening rhythm on a wooden chair seat. After two bars Florence came in like a marauding bear. Cornet shock chords stabbed the startled air. It was just picking up atmosphere when the soprano came in with the counter-melody; very loud, very high and very sharp. The girl could read well, but did she have an ear?

"All right," Lucy stopped them. "Let's have a tune-up."

"Tune-up?" Rachel the flugel horn player looked alarmed.

"What do you want? Advance warning?" said Florence, flexing her slide and taking advantage of the stoppage to glance through her part for anything that might cause the player concern.

Lucy glared at them to be quiet. She did not want to offend the newcomer. So she went round each player, making her blow a C and was a bit depressed to hear how many and various were the C's to be had, when subjected to solo scrutiny. But at least she was able to persuade Charmaine, as the soprano player was called, to pull out her slide half an inch without it looking as though she were being singled out.

At the break, Lucy quietly thanked Ruth for her gift.

"It's the least of what I owe you, Lucy."

"How did you know there was going to be a soprano?"

"I didn't. I've got it cued into my part and I was hoping to play it myself. You know how I love high notes." She pulled a rueful face.

"What did you have in mind for percussion?"

"I'm glad you mentioned that. I know you've been looking for a drummer for some time. I think I may have found you one."

"You never!"

"I don't know what her name is, I'm afraid. I don't even know if she can read sheet music. She plays with a group called Raggle Taggle and I'm told they hang out at the Black Cat on Saturdays."

"Which Black Cat is that?"

"The Horwich side of Blackrod. Just off the bypass I think."

"Blackrod? There's nowt there bar about three streets and a pub."

"Well anyway, she plays really well, so if you want to get in touch with the management, I'm sure they'll be helpful." Ruth had done her homework. She intended to leave the rest to Lucy. "It's entirely up to you. I just thought you might be interested."

"Worth a try, I suppose," said Lucy, not relishing the idea of phoning a complete stranger. "Could you ask her, do you think?"

"It'd be much better coming from you," Ruth pointed out and went outside for a smoke.

She lit up and shook the match until the flame gave up the ghost then threw it into the nearby brook. She drew on her cigarette. A piece of moon was etched across with the silhouette of leaves. There was still a coral tinge in the west, legacy of the departed sun. The tender spring leaves whispered in a gentle stir of air.

She was a fool. What was she looking for? More pain? Had the affair with Sarah taught her so little? Would it be better if nothing came of this and the band battled on without percussion? Or could she easily forget those blue eyes which had locked onto hers over the moving stream of humanity?

Poised in these bitter-sweet reflections, she noticed Annette picking her way in high heels across the rough parking space to join her.

"What a lovely evening!"

"Yes. Just look at the colour of that sky!"

Annette broke off a stem of rye grass and began pulling the head to bits.

"We saw you on the telly."

"Managed not to blink, then?"

"The kids thought you were terrific."

"It's nice to please the under tens."

"Tim's eleven," Annette corrected her, "and Harold is even older."

"Did Harold watch it?" asked Ruth in surprise.

"Some of it. He asked me to find out if anything was going to come of it."

"I wouldn't have thought he'd be interested."

"He's probably put a bet on it."

"Oh! That makes sense. Well you can tell him from me that something is going to come of it."

"Really?"

"Yes really." Ruth paused, savouring the moment. "There's a film company wants to do a programme on us."

"What do you mean, 'us'? All the bands?"

"No. Just the Stonemasons. It's an independent company but they're doing it for a TV series to be called '*Beat Around Britain*'. They've been commissioned to cover the North West and they chose us for this area on the strength of our performance in Manchester. They're going to film us at the Granary and edit the result into some sort of documentary."

"Ye gods! That's fame!" There was envy in Annette's voice.

27

"I don't want fame," said Ruth and she meant it. "A rise in our booking fee would satisfy me."

"My news is going to sound a bit tame after that."

"News? You've got news?" She glanced at Annette's slender frame, rounded only in the right places. "You can't be pregnant again."

"You're right. I can't. I'm applying for a job."

"First trumpet at the Liverpool Phil?"

"Don't be sarcastic." Annette swung her mane over her shoulder in a gesture of pique. "It's in beauty culture. I wish I hadn't told you now."

"That's perfect. For you. Assuming you've anything to learn in that direction."

"I've got an interview on Friday. Wish me luck."

"You don't need it. Only a cross-eyed misogynist with a migraine could turn you down."

All pique vanished. Ruth was forgiven. Annette had recently passed the big three-O watershed. Anno domini loomed on her horizon – as yet no bigger than a man's hand. Compliments were needed as never before.

She had to content herself with the ego boost she had been given, though, for before she could milk any more from Ruth, the sound of *Come to the Cookhouse Door* played on a bass trombone reached their ears. It was the signal for straying players that Lucy was ready to start again. Ruth hastily ground out her cigarette and they made their way back to the band-room in a mutually supportive state of mind.

4

Lucy was not a person to let the grass grow under her feet. The ground which Ruth had opened up for her was not going to be left to lie fallow. She sowed it with the seeds of her own research, then with a couple of carefully thought-out phone calls she watered the furrows. As a result the green shoots of growth appeared the following week in the form of an unfamiliar van which was parked outside the band room.

The vehicle was quite different from the ancient rust-heap that the trombone-playing sisters used. It was last year's make and the words *Raggle* and *Taggle* were jauntily displayed over its sides and rear doors, in all the colours of the rainbow. There was a professional neatness, however, about the apparently random distribution of paint.

Ruth gave three silent cheers as she drove her Hillman into what space was left and climbed out. She extracted her handbag and the cornet from the passenger seat, locked her car and turned towards the hall, hardly able to believe that her strategy had been so successful, while resolving not to push her luck by showing too much interest in the newcomer.

But it was impossible not to notice that something was happening. As soon as she set foot on the stone step of the doorway she nearly collided with an older man who was on his way out to the van. Having escaped that disaster, she had to leap aside to avoid being mown down by a younger one whose view was obscured by the bass drum he was carrying into the band room a few steps behind her.

The young lady with the short fair hair and blue eyes was already occupying a substantial area of floor space. She instructed her beasts of burden where to put the objects as they brought them in. She slotted in this and screwed in that, until her percussion centre was ready. Then she seated herself amidst a variety of equipment, which included not just top hat and snare drum with bass drum and triangle, but a whole array of graduated tam-tams and a large cymbal for solitary smiting. Affixed to the rim of the bass drum were cowbell, triangle, a wood block, a small cymbal and several temple blocks, or 'skulls'. Laid out on a nearby chair were castanets, maracas, claves and a tambourine. All within reach of her small limbs.

The trombone transport could be heard rattling into the parking lot. It was a rusty old van with the peeling legend *Bill Ainscough's Hot Stompers* still legible along its sides. Their father, it was easy to guess, had been a professional trombonist.

"Well I'll be tarred and feathered!" Florence was heard to bellow to the accompaniment of much door-slamming.

"Not in our house, you won't," responded Gladys as the sisters strode in. The manifestation before them brought them to an abrupt halt. Their mouths clamped shut in the effort not to comment.

The older man, who sported a draconian short back and sides for a haircut, put down a box of sticks, brushes and other accoutrements for hitting with. He straightened up and surveyed the room full of women.

"Which one of you is Mrs Brindle?" he clipped.

Lucy stepped forwards, wondering whether to bring her heels together and salute.

"You're Major Prescott-Withers?"

"Just call me Prescott. Everybody does."

They shook hands.

"Thank you for bringing your daughter. I'm sure she'll make a valuable addition to our band."

"Glad to help. Pick her up at twenty-one fifty-five, right?"

"Yes. No – er – yes," faltered Lucy.

"Thanks a lot, Daddy. See you," said the drummer in the tone of voice that young adults use when they want a parent to take themselves off before they become an even greater embarrassment.

There was a bit of a silence when the Major had gone, because everybody was busy not saying what sprang to mind. Teenagers Rachel and Rebecca nudged one another and put their hands in front of their mouths, imagining that this concealed their smirks. Annette sat with a slightly sour face assessing Daddy's income from the quality of the new arrival's clothes. Ruth watched guardedly and without comment.

"What a lot of drums!" It took young Wendy on second cornet to voice the thought. "Are you going to play all of those?"

"That's what they're there for."

The newcomer was not insensitive to atmosphere. Though she had abounding self-confidence, she could not help feeling a little strange.

Lucy came to her aid.

"I want you all to welcome Cheryl to the band," she began. "She has kindly agreed to come and play percussion for us which, as you all know, is a long-felt need. We hope you'll like us, Cheryl, and feel thoroughly at home. I know I can rely on you all to make Cheryl feel at home," she added, giving them all a meaningful glare.

Eileen on solo horn loyally murmured her assent. She even turned around to shake hands with Cheryl, who was stationed directly behind her. The others added similar gestures and

Cheryl began to wish that they could just start playing and get on with it.

Lucy brought over a sheaf of percussion parts and looked for somewhere to put them. One thing was missing from that welter of equipment – a music stand.

"Sorry. I haven't used one of those since I was at school."

Cheryl made it sound as though only babies used music stands.

"You do read music?"

"Oh yes. I can read music."

Lucy gazed around the room for something she could utilise instead. All she could see were chairs. They were too low and too bulky.

Ruth came to her rescue by passing her own stand over the heads of the horns.

"You can borrow mine for tonight," she said.

Cheryl smiled her thanks and, as their eyes met, Ruth was pleased to note a flash of recognition, before Lucy's twin-set and pearls cut across her line of vision. Cheryl had remembered her. She turned to Annette.

"Can I share your stand?"

"Provided you behave yourself."

"You drive a hard bargain."

"We'll start with a march," announced Lucy, having succeeded in finding a spot to put the stand where Cheryl could read from it.

"*Men of Manchester.*"

Cheryl found the page and pushed the sleeves of her sweater half way up her forearms. She selected two sticks and they fell into her hands as if they belonged there. The cornets gave the opening fanfare. The others joined in, but you could hardly tell because of the tremendous noise that was coming from cymbal and drums. The horns froze like rabbits caught in the headlights of a car. Lucy was so distracted she lost her place, but it did not matter, because the beat was so strong that she could have flung her baton down on the floor and walked out and the rest of the band would have carried on regardless in perfect time.

She stopped them, though it took some pretty dogged rapping on her stand before she could make herself heard.

"Much, much less volume, Cheryl."

They retraced their steps over the opening of *Men of Manchester* and it was better, but not better enough. She had to stop them once more. She made up her mind that she would continue to stop them for however long it took until Cheryl got it right. Start as you mean to go on; that was her motto.

"About half that volume, Cheryl. Listen for the euphonium, will you, and make sure you can hear it above the drums."

It took two more stoppages but in the end she had the dynamic where she wanted it. She even tried increasing it towards the end and bringing it down again. As she suspected, she could not quite bring it down far enough, but she was sure that with a little more work she would. There was no doubt that with a drummer they sounded much more like the kind of sound she was accustomed to hearing in the park on Sunday afternoons in the summer, a 'real' band in fact. When they broke for a rest at mid practice she smiled at Cheryl and told her that she was very pleased to have her in the band.

Ruth came across in the hope of introducing herself and perhaps having a chat about the rock concert. But there were too many others pushing in for the privilege. As well as Lucy, Florence was keen to have a word. Young Wendy was hopping up and down in her eagerness to have a go at cow bell and skulls.

The time was not ripe. So Ruth went outside for a smoke.

She sat on the low wall by the parking space, which the stream ran along before disappearing underground. She tapped her ash into the water and heard it hiss. Soon Annette appeared and sat on the other end of the wall, elegantly, as though posing for a photograph. It was not affected. She was naturally graceful.

"What do you think of Madam?" she wanted to know.

"Worth waiting for, wasn't she."

"As a player, perhaps, when she lets us hear ourselves."

"Well we don't know her as a person, do we?" said Ruth a little irritably.

Annette was disappointed. She had been looking forward to a good bitching session. But then a thought occurred to her.

"Do you fancy her, or something?"

"Don't be so crass, Annette," snapped Ruth. She picked up a lump of moss and hurled it in the direction of what looked like a frog, but turned out to be a bit of leaf. The moss floated back down towards her, twirled around in an eddy and disappeared into the black tunnel under the wall.

"I didn't mean to hurt your feelings. Sorry."

"No need to be sorry," conceded Ruth. "You're right of course. She does attract me. I don't know why. But then does one ever?"

"Strange. I find her quite obnoxious. Good job we're not all the same, I suppose."

"Some of us are a bit too different for comfort," observed Ruth sadly.

"Come for a drink at the Black Horse afterwards?" suggested Annette, in an attempt to stop her drifting back into morbid territory.

"What's the point, Annette? The sight of you would only bring an army of fellers."

"Don't you ever feel tempted to give the fellers a try?"

Ruth gave her a heavy-lidded stare, like a lizard's.

"None whatsoever. That's the trouble."

There was not a lot more to say after that. They jumped down from the wall and wandered slowly back towards the hall, about six feet separating them, as if to emphasise the gulf between their situations.

After the practice Ruth retrieved her music stand, hoping for at least a bit of conversation with the drummer she had gone to such trouble to enlist. But the Major was there, chivvying proceedings along. So Ruth was rewarded by the briefest of thanks before wending her solitary way home to her empty house. She had left the lounge light switched on, to deter any burglars, but the hall was dark. It was cold. The rooms mocked her with their emptiness. A deafening silence greeted her from the bedroom when she flung her cornet and coat onto the bed. A double bed, but only half slept in.

She escaped to the kitchen, where at least the fridge was humming, and turned on the radio rather loud. She made herself a sandwich and some coffee and sat and stared at the washing machine and stared at the picture on the wall. It was an abstract and it could mean anything or nothing, depending on how you felt when you viewed it. At the moment it meant nothing. It belonged to the landlord.

Should she get a dog?

"Hi there. Rover?"

He would come bounding over joyfully and lick her face, whining with pleasure and demanding a brisk walk.

It would not be fair. Dogs need company. She was hardly ever in.

How she wished she had gone to the Black Horse with Annette!

She switched off the radio, took out her guitar and began to strum a few minor chords, to match her mood. She hit upon a descending sequence that really took her fancy. Like her spirits, it was going down. She tried it again. She wanted to see how far she could take the progression before returning to the home key. Too far, really. Too far for popular music. It could still be used in the introduction, though. What about words?

"*Never felt so bad,*" she sang to herself. "*Got it bad as I've ever had. 'Cos I'm taking a ride – on the slippery slide – to the pit of a depression and there's nowhere to hide.* No – wait. Can't sing that. Too many syllables. How about – *to that dangerous spot* – no – *to that murky black pit with nothing inside* – no, that doesn't make sense. *back to that place where I so nearly died* – Hm. I don't think so."

She altered a note here and there, reworked some of the words, ran it through and improved on the chords, added a second verse, then went to bed an hour and a half later one song the richer and lighter of heart.

But when she gave it to the boys at their weekly get-together, the reaction was predictable.

"Going down down down? Who's going to listen to that? Why not going up up up?" argued Donny.

"The word 'up' doesn't fit the mood of the song."

"Rising high, high, high. How about that?"

"Wouldn't that be too explicit? I mean in its implications?"

Donny gave one of his dirty little laughs.

"Nothing can be too explicit for pop music."

"That's how we like it," chipped in Ron. "Explicit."

"We can try 'rising high' next time if it pleases you," Ruth told him in a tone of forced tolerance. "But we can't put it to this tune. This tune goes down. You can't sing 'rising high' when the tune is going down."

"The whole thing is just so damn miserable. Look at the opening. 'Never felt so bad'. Who wants to hear a thing like that?"

"Somebody should have told Duke Ellington about that."

"I've never seen his name in the charts."

Ruth sighed.

"Oh well, if you don't like it, that's that I suppose."

"I like it," Ricky broke in for the first time. "Listen! After that last bit, how about if I do this?" and he added a striking glissando down to bottom E.

"Hey, that's groovy!" approved Ron. "Do it again."

He did. It was.

"Well then we'll do some work on it tonight if we get through all the other stuff okay," Donny conceded, finding himself outnumbered. "Maybe we'll try it out on Saturday. If it goes down like a concrete balloon, we'll let it sink without trace."

The Granary was on the outskirts of a village which boasted a population of about two hundred. An old tithe barn, it stood apart from any dwellings, except for the adjoining living quarters of the caretaker, and was surrounded by lofty beech trees of great beauty. The brook which ran down from the moors passed close by. A previous owner had diverted some of it to form an ornamental pond, studded with bulrushes.

During the war soldiers had been billeted there. The main area had been used as a food store. Barbed wire had kept at bay curiosity seekers, but it had not deterred the rats. At the end of the war it had stood derelict long enough for all the windows to have been broken by stone-throwing vandals.

It was not until the fifties that an enterprising caterer from Adlington had acquired the lease and turned it into tea rooms. Once the barn area was cleared, exposing a fine wooden floor, the idea of holding dances there was irresistible. Although few people lived nearby, there were plenty of industrial towns in the vicinity. The age of the motor car was dawning, and here there was a huge area of parking space. It was an idea whose time had come.

Its enormous roof was covered in stone shingles. Supporting this immense weight, the cross-raftered oak beams descended in arches into huge boulders on the edge of the dance area. The girls could stand and lean against the stone while waiting to be invited to dance. A bar was set up at one end, a dais on the other. Tables were placed between the stone supports. When music was provided on a Saturday night, the word quickly spread around Horwich and Chorley, Adlington and Westhoughton, Bolton, Bury, Blackburn, Darwen, Wigan and Leigh.

It became *the* place to go on a Saturday night.

The black beams, which curved down into the stone, must have been silent witnesses to many strange sights over a century or two or three. But whatever merry-making may have taken place it could hardly have subjected them to the fumes, the cigarette smoke, the throb of many engines or the pounding that came from the amplifiers such as were now current. By ten o'clock the floor was packed with dancers and the event was in full swing.

The Stonemasons were shortly to take a break and let the disc-jockey have half an hour's fun. It was a good time to throw in an untried item and see if it could swim.

"Right," shouted Donny taking a quick drag from the cigarette he kept smouldering away on a nearby ashtray to draw upon between numbers, the drifting smoke threatening to catch at the throats of the vocalisers. "We'll try *Going Down*."

Ron seized the microphone and announced that they were going to do one more number then would have a little break and be back soon, "So don't go away, folks."

Then Ruth played her chord sequence on the keyboard, giving the signal to Donny, who responded with a light rise and fall of the cymbal and two rim shots to lead in the lyric.

She took the main vocal part herself, since Ron needed more than one practice to pitch his entry right and to get familiar with the words.

'Never felt this bad,' she sang,
'Got it bad as I've ever had
And I'm taking a ride
On the slippery slide,
I couldn't get off, however I tried.'

'Couldn't get off the slippery slide,
No matter how you tried,' sang Ron and Ricky softly.

'Going down, down, down,' she continued.

'Down, down, down,' added Ricky's tenor voice.

'Down, down, down, down, DOWN.' concluded Ron in his best baritone.

Ricky then finished off each verse with a glissando down to the bottom E of his bass guitar.

After many repetitions of this process, everybody in the room knew it as well as they did, and most people like music which they know, better than that with which they are not familiar. So at the end they applauded wildly.

Exhilarated by this success, the Stonemasons headed for the side room where they could be served at a little bar, away from the crush. Pushing through the crowd, Ruth felt her arm detained by a hand. She turned to find herself looking into Cheryl's blue eyes at very close range.

"I liked your last number," said the soft pink mouth.

"You and a few others, I think."

"Write it yourself?"

"All except that last glissando. That was Ricky's idea."

"It's good," persisted Cheryl. "I wish I could write songs like that."

Ruth wondered whether she could bear to get involved again. Or whether she could bear not to.

"I'm just off for a drink," she said. "You with anybody?"

"I came with Barney, but I think he's found himself some talent."

"Tough luck."

"Not really. He's my kid brother."

"Then in that case we can leave him to his own devices and desires. Come on. Join the inner circle."

She ushered her by the elbow through the door, marvelling at the powerful effect of contact with the right person, which was probably what Cheryl was marvelling about too, in a different way. Ricky bought them each a mysterious concoction which he called a Granary Special in sinister tones and for his pains was kept in the background as the two women launched into a discussion of the problems of finding material and of arranging it and the prospects of getting bookings and the merits of various venues. Eventually the boys decided it was time to break them up. Donny had been eying Cheryl speculatively for some time. Although she was small and feminine, there was a toughness about her that lay just below the surface.

He muscled his way between them.

"You've just missed the TV man, Anderton," he told Ruth. "Too bad."

"Was he here?"

"He wants us to do *Going Down*," Ron told her.

"For the cameras?"

"What's this?" butted in Cheryl unwisely.

Donny rested his hand on that part of the bar between the two females and, turning his back on Ruth, leaned close to the younger woman.

"What Sunday School did you spring from, then?"

"She plays drums with Raggle Taggle," Ruth told him irritably.

"Never heard of them." Ron put his oar in, coming up close on Cheryl's other side so that she was hemmed in by the two men.

"It's that spotty lot from Horwich." Donny told him.

"Can't be much good if you can't get a booking for a Saturday night. Come to pick up a few tips, have you?"

"Maybe."

Cheryl was not going to confess that Raggle Taggle had had their venue usurped by a wedding party for the evening.

"Leave her alone, Donny," Ruth realised that her cause would be lost in these circumstances, but she had to try and defend it. She failed to get past his arm. Cheryl moved away and tried to walk round to Ruth's side, but Donny turned and barred her way.

"Wotcher got, then?" he persisted. "Two bongos and a dustbin lid?"

"She's got a better kit than you have," Ruth snapped at him, letting her exasperation show.

"What a waste," Donny sneered.

"Who *is* this gentleman?" Cheryl addressed Ruth in her best cut glass tones. She had discovered that an imitation of her old headmistress usually repelled difficult people.

Predictably, Donny and Ron fell about with "Oh I say!" and "My name is Lady Muck!" in silly voices. But they did back off a couple of steps in the process.

As always, it was Ricky who came to the rescue, before the banter became a slanging match.

"I think it's time we went back," he butted in, pushing his way between the opposing parties. "It'll take us about ten minutes to beat a path through that crowd."

So the Stonemasons pushed their way back and resumed the stage, where Ruth made a resolution to keep Donny out of her social hair in future.

The manager was waiting by the dais.

"I've had six people ask if you'll play that last number again."

Two people had asked Donny the same thing just on his way back from the toilet. So he had to give it the thumbs-up. Ron did a bit of spiel into the microphone about popular request for our newly-minted number and the audience cheered! The Stonemasons went down down down all over again and the crowd loved it.

5

One Sunday, summer paid an advance visit. It was the kind of day that May can produce when it is in a good mood. Tender green leaves decked the hedgerows and the banks were pink and yellow with campion and primrose; the woods carpeted with bluebells. Hundreds of people packed their families into cars or crowded into the bus and headed for the Rivington countryside.

Ruth drove to the sheep-quiet slopes of Anglezarke, seated herself none too comfortably on a bit of dry stone wall with a good view over the Rivington reservoirs. She lit a cigarette. Dotted here and there across the panorama were other people enjoying the day. Sometimes a young man and woman strolled along with their arms around one another or hand in hand. A few shoals of boys on bicycles drifted around yelling to one another.

But most of mankind was clustered in family groups. She had passed a few along the road; father and mother and offspring of all shapes and sizes. Sometimes they included a dog or a grandparent or a supernumerary aunt. She glimpsed them on the paths, in the fields, picnicking on the grass above the reservoir.

That was Sarah's world now; the one she had opted for.

She could blend back into humankind, indistinguishable among the crowd. There would be no more offensive stares, no more half-concealed smirks or obstructionism from petty officialdom. Who could blame her? Was that not what they were made for, the female of the species? To marry and have children?

She climbed off the gritty stone, laid her jacket on the grass and settled more comfortably. Soon her cigarette was becoming short and she looked for an area of ground into which she could safely grind out the remains. But the more closely she examined the turf around her the more she began to discover that she was not as alone as she had imagined. She was at the centre of a whole world of minute life. One careless gesture on her part could bring disaster to law-abiding creatures whose rightful territory this was.

From a tiny hole by her coat sleeve the ants appeared, clambering over dead stems and any obstacles that blocked their path. What lay at the end of this journey appeared to be just another hole, but it must have been important to them. Other ants were making the same trip in the opposite direction. When they ran into one another they went into frantic semaphore. Were they transmitting messages? What could they be saying to one another?

"Anthony's just found the remains of a half-eaten pear. Get there quick or it'll all be gone."

Most of them had a sense of purpose, but one had lost his way and wandered with feebly flapping feelers, scrambling over a dead leaf, pausing and waving antennae as if trying to catch a friendly signal. Was it a scout doing a reconnoitre, or did ants too have their outsiders?

The beetles were cumbersome by comparison. They would climb onto slim stems that bent under their weight, turning the creature turtle as a result. That was a serious matter for a beetle. He would lie on his back flailing his legs to catch hold of anything by which he might right himself. If there was nothing within reach he could flail until he died.

One such fell onto her coat in that manner and lay like a capsized boat, its desperate little feet not waving, but drowning. She gave him a helping hand by flicking him upright with her finger nail. He scuttled over the hem and dug himself back into the matted turf.

The cigarette was burning her fingers. She threw it onto the road. Then she turned over and lay on her stomach. Even the most pernicious weeds displayed beautiful flowers when seen from such close range. There was thistle and clover, sorrel and burdock. A cluster of plantains lifted their fat heads on their long, tough stems. If you were the size of a vole they would resemble triffids, stuck around with stamens, the pollen heads like the feet of Micky Mouse, making a pale halo. It was a world in miniature to which she did not belong.

Yet she felt a closer affinity to it than she did to the blank faces that peered out at her from the windows of passing cars. It had a permanency that transcended the restless melting pot of humanity. It would cope with discarded half-eaten fruit in the garden, or crumbs on the lino of a kitchen floor; whichever came its way.

A cold gust of wind riffled through the hair on the back of her neck. She lifted her head towards the western horizon. The sun had gone in. A curtain of grey had risen, perfectly horizontal at the top, to close the show. That was the end of the summer preview. To her left the sky was a threatening shade of slate.

She rose, shook her coat and made for the car.

Because of the feeling of isolation which had held her in its grip since Sarah left, the Wednesday band nights had become important to her. Lucy needed her expertise on the cornet. They all did. She had a role and it was one which brought her a degree of inclusion. She went along the following week with more to look forward to than the mere pleasure of playing. She would have colleagues with whom to exchange greetings. And Cheryl would be there.

She strode into the familiar room where Florence was filling the air with the sound of lip-slurs. That was how she warmed up each week. She would start on a low F and work her way up the scale. Like Ruth, she took her playing seriously. Her two sisters on first and second trombone preferred to swap gossip as they opened their music stands and assembled their instruments.

Judith the repiano cornet player was chatting to Lucy. They were both music teachers and there was always something to remark upon about the curriculum. The Raggle Taggle van arrived and its cargo of percussion was borne in piecemeal by Cheryl's line of coolies. Cheryl gave Ruth a little wave and a big smile.

"Been busy over the weekend then, have you?" she heard Annette murmer at her side.

"Shut up!" snarled Ruth through gently smiling teeth.

Cheryl soon had her drums in order and her cohorts dismissed. The band rattled through familiar numbers which they hardly needed to rehearse at all. By this time the piece which Ruth had supplied them with for Florence's benefit was the only one which had not been played to exhaustion.

The first thing Lucy did when they took their half-time knitting break was to remind them of the Sale of Work which was to take place shortly. It was being held in order to raise money for the band, she told them; money which was to be used in particular to purchase more pieces of music. If they could find several works which suited the band as well as *Black Rock Bay*, they could set up a programme fit to gladden the ears of any audience.

Ruth had not volunteered for any particular stall, but she was not going to be allowed to escape. As the ladies dispersed to their corners Lucy collared her.

"I've got no one to be a stall-holder on the book stall. Can you do it?"

"I think so. I suppose so. Yes of course." she agreed, reminding herself that it was better to be asked than to be left out.

"How much more music would you say we need?"

"Lots," said Ruth and saw Lucy's face fall. "But not necessarily all at once."

"I was hoping for enough to buy at least three pieces. It's pricey to get a full score and all the parts. Not like buying piano music."

"I know."

"So it's very important to choose carefully, don't you think?"

"Oh absolutely."

"I was planning to go to the Music Centre in Wythenshaw."

"Just outside Manchester, is that?"

"Yes. I want to have a good old look round. You can never tell what you're getting from catalogues, can you."

"They can be quite a good guide."

"Yes but it's not like actually holding a score in your hand and leafing through, is it? Will you come with me?"

"Oh! Yes." Ruth was quite pleased to find her company wanted. "If you let me know in advance when you're going."

"I'll speak to you again after the sale, then."

Lucy made her next bee-line for Cheryl, which forestalled Ruth from the same port of call. Never mind. She wanted a cigarette.

She went outside into the parking area. The evenings were getting lighter. There was a bit of wind and a feeling it would rain as soon as look at you. But a particularly operatic thrush was taking advantage of the dampness in the air, which gave its voice extra carrying power, by serenading its mate from somewhere high in a tree. Ruth jumped onto the stone wall and put one foot up and let the other leg hang over the side for balance, while she let the sound wash over her.

"Shhhh!" she cautioned when Annette came to join her.

Annette parked herself sedately by a stone pillar a couple of yards away along the wall. Her hair glowed in the twilight as a shaft of light from the setting sun sneaked out from under a westerly bank of cloud and painted her gold. Her limbs were disposed as gracefully as a cat's. The sight of her was a treat for the eye.

Why, then, did Ruth's heart not lift as it did when Cheryl so much as walked into the room? Because she was falling victim to the same old foolishness. That was why. Well this time she would be wiser. She would snap out of it right now.

"I got the job," Annette's voice broke into her thoughts.

"Congratulations! But then, I knew you would."

"It means I have to go away for training."

"Training? You need training to be beautiful?"

"To teach beauty care, idiot."

Ruth felt a pang. Sarah used to call her idiot. Quite often. It was little things like that which continued to catch her unawares and hurt.

"Guess where I'm going?" persevered Annette. She could see Ruth was unhappy. Was she envious?

"I can't imagine," said Ruth flatly. "Ashton in Makerfield?"

"Paris. London and Paris."

"Paris! Of all the luck! Can you speak French?"

"Well… school French. I could. Years ago."

Too many years.

"You'll come back a different person," said Ruth, her mouth turning down. "You'll be too grand for the likes of us."

"Too grand for the famous Ruth Anderton? That'll be the day."

Ruth said nothing. She flung the remains of her cigarette into the brook, where it landed with a hiss. She wanted to say that she wished Annette would not go. But that would be selfish.

"I'm very pleased for you," she got out at last. "I hope you have fun."

"Fun? Who said anything about fun? This is going to be very hard work and study."

"Of course," Ruth smiled. "In Paris."

"People do work in Paris," Annette pointed out, accurately, though not earnestly. She descended carefully from the wall. "Come on. I can hear Lucy rapping for order from here."

Ruth jumped down and they made their way back inside.

As soon as all the ladies were re-seated, with their instruments at the ready, Lucy gave the order: "Regimental Selection!"

There followed the usual chorus of groans.

"I don't know why you all complain," she observed. "This is a right good piece for brass."

"Let's face it, Lucy," said Gladys in her best whine, "It hasn't got much woman-appeal."

"We're not playing it because it's appealing, we're playing it…"

"Because it's appalling," cut in Ruth as she placed the part on her stand and picked up her cornet.

So Lucy had her revenge by breaking the piece up into sections and taking the difficult bits separately. Ruth had to sit and listen whilst the weaker sisters were made to go over the runs which they had been accustomed to fudging. Individuals were singled out to play by themselves, so nobody was able to hide behind someone else's greater expertise.

But when at the end they played it straight through all together it sounded much better.

In line with her resolution not to get foolish again, Ruth had intended to walk straight out after the practice, but Cheryl called her over.

"Want to give us a hand here?"

The Major and Barney had not yet arrived. So Ruth could not easily refuse, even though Sally-the-bass, whose address Annette had had such difficulty finding, was already dismantling some of the drum kit. Sally was now transported in the Raggle Taggle van, because of the size of her instrument and the direction of her home. She was happier with this arrangement, since Cheryl was more punctual than Annette. So she did not mind being landed with the task of putting various parts of the drum kit by the door, ready for the men when they arrived with the van.

Ruth tackled the things she knew she could do, such as folding up the music stand which Cheryl now possessed.

"Have you been filmed yet?" asked Cheryl, trying to sound casual.

"No, not yet," Ruth told her. "Friday's the day, weather permitting."

"Weather? You're being shot outside?" interrupted Sally, as she picked up the side drum and its stand.

"Don't make it sound like a firing squad."

"It's just that I thought they had studios for that kind of thing."

"Some of it, yes. Some of it will be studio-taped. The fact is that they liked the Granary so much they wanted to take some footage with the building in the background. It's an architectural rarity, apparently."

"Can anybody come and watch?" asked Cheryl, detaching her large cymbal and laying it gently in its case.

Ruth smiled.

"Provided they don't get too close to Donny, they can. Very discreetly, you know, and without getting themselves noticed."

"I could bring the van and help you carry stuff if you need it."

"The Stonemasons have their own van."

"Oh yes. Of course they would have."

She sounded disappointed. Ruth took pity on her.

"I suppose you could just sort of happen to be passing...

49

admiring the scenery, you know. They sell tea and coffee and soft drinks at the Granary during the day."

"Good idea. What time are you due there? Morning or afternoon?"

"Both. As long as there's daylight. Oh and for goodness sake don't turn up in that fancy van of yours. They'll see you coming a mile away."

"But it's my only transport."

"Get the Rivington bus. Number 312. It goes regularly every two hours. From the Crown in Horwich."

"Every two hours!"

"Yes. I'll run you back afterwards."

At that point the Major and Barney arrived, which put an end to the conversation. Ruth picked up her cornet and made for her car. There was a cheer from the Hot Stompers van. It had been trapped in a corner by the Raggle Taggle van, but would have room to manoeuvre when Ruth's Hillman Minx was removed from the scene.

'So much for snapping out of it,' thought Ruth as she drove home.

On Friday the weather was far from ideal, but shooting went ahead in fits and starts. After they had had to break off for the third time, Ruth retired to one of the wooden seats outside the Granary to study the schedule, when Cheryl materialised from her discreet station in the porch and sat beside her. She was sensibly dressed in jeans. A haversack was slung over her shoulder. Her clothes were shades of dull green and brown. She must have taken the suggestion to blend into the background literally.

"Hi!" she said.

Ruth looked up from the papers she was holding and smiled.

"Nobody's asked you what you're doing here, then?"

"I haven't given anybody the chance."

"You became part of the scenery?"

"I've just made a bag of crisps and a lemonade last an hour."

Ruth knew then that she was not going to snap out of it. She gazed across towards the pasture land, where a magpie made a dipping flight from one high beech to another. How uncomplicated it was to be a magpie.

Cheryl picked up a round pebble and started throwing it in the air and catching it. She was the sort of person who finds it hard to keep still.

"Is it going to stay fine?" she mused, screwing her eyes up towards the western horizon, whose aspect was not promising.

"I think not. They've already had to break off once or twice and there's a big fat cloud up there, waiting to pounce."

A large van packed with equipment stood in the middle of the huge parking area. Men hovered around its open back doors like wasps at the entrance to their nest. Light meters had to be re-checked from one minute to the next. It was a blustery day.

The director had found an ancient cairn which he felt would make a good background for some shots; the Stonemasons seated on it at various levels; the Stonemasons running past it; the Stonemasons looming up to it from the dip behind, hidden by grass from the waist down; the Stonemasons standing in front of it. Oh yes. It had possibilities.

The trouble was that the ground was covered in tough turfs with boggy bits in between. One camera man had already fallen over backwards. A break had been called. The boys had gone to the loo and Ruth had seated herself on the bench with a copy of the schedule to work out just how much longer they were likely to be kept here.

That was when Cheryl had chosen her moment to emerge from hiding.

"Let's grab a coffee while we can," suggested Ruth.

"I've got a flask. Want some?"

"You haven't!"

Ruth watched in surprise as Cheryl opened her haversack and extracted two plastic cups and a flask.

"There's milk in it," Cheryl told her. "I hope you want milk."

"If it's hot and it's wet it'll do."

She clasped her hands around the cup and took a sip. Of course it was good coffee.

"So how did you get to be a drummer?" she asked. "Accident or design?"

"Oh design. Definitely. I've always been fascinated by drums. But of course I never got the chance to try them until uncle Digby gave Barney a set for his sixth birthday."

"I bet your uncle Digby wasn't very popular with your parents."

"Daddy was in Aden then, so it didn't affect him. In any case Barney only bashed them about a bit for a week, then he lost interest and took to his new bicycle instead. That was my chance."

"He let you play them?"

"He couldn't stop me. I was ten. Bigger than him."

"But you've had training. I can tell you've had training. Did your mother think you had such promise that she sent you for lessons?"

"No fear. She sent me to a boarding school on the South Coast. It was the only way to separate me from the drum set."

"So what happened?"

"They had a good music department. My mother gave them strict instructions that I was to be taught to play the violin. So I learned to play the violin. I hated it. There's no rhythm in a violin."

"Oh I don't know. What about…?"

"Anyway, I managed to wangle a place on the percussion. It wasn't difficult. They were always asking for volunteers. Then I had some proper coaching from a professional."

"Didn't your parents know?"

"Not at first. Not until they came to a school concert. By that time the school depended on me. They didn't want to lose me. So Mummy and Daddy relented. Then Daddy left the army and went into partnership with a friend who had this stockbroker's business in Bolton. I was transferred to Bolton School and lived at home."

"Did you lose your drums?"

"For a time. But when I was coming up to eighteen and everybody asked what I wanted for my birthday, I told them cymbals, side-drums and all the various bits. That's all the stuff I use in band. More coffee?"

"If there is some." Ruth held out her cup.

"That's my story, now you can tell me yours."

Just then Ricky rounded the corner of the building and came across to advise as to the next move.

"They want us over in that field, for some reason." Ricky told her. "They like that line of tall trees, I think. They want us to play."

"Where do we plug in?"

"We don't. They add the sound later."

"Can I come and watch you?" Cheryl asked.

"Better stay here," Ricky told her quite kindly. "Otherwise you're likely to get an earful from Mister Big."

He meant the director. He gestured Ruth to follow him and when they had gone a little way he dropped his voice.

"Don't get me wrong, Ruth, but you'd better watch that girl. Donny says she's on the make."

"He's probably right."

Ricky turned and glanced at her as they continued to walk side by side. Her face was impassive, but he knew exactly what the score was.

"It doesn't make any difference, though, does it?"

"No Ricky. It doesn't make the slightest difference."

After the shooting, Cheryl hopped into Ruth's car and they drove away together as the three men watched.

"I see the Anderton pervert has brought her latest girlie-pal again," sneered Donny and he spat on the ground.

"It's none of our business," said Ricky.

Donny glared at him.

"She plays drums. And she's too damn pushy!" he snarled. "Where are you going?"

But Ricky climbed into his car and drove away.

That evening the Prescott-Withers telephone rang.

"It's for you, Cheryl." The exasperation could be heard in the Major's voice. He was expecting an important call from Scotland. "Try to keep it short, chicken."

Cheryl picked up the antique phone, which was situated in a room furnished with antiques. The voice belonged to Donny Mason.

"I've got two tickets for Five and a Half tonight. Want to come?"

Five and a Half were one of the top groups and were particularly noted for their unconventional percussion effects.

"I thought they were in Preston tonight?"

"They are."

"Me and a couple of friends are going to see them next week when they're in Bolton."

"Just as you like. I'll take someone else. I just thought you might like to meet Phil Zombie, you being a drummer, like."

There was a stunned pause.

"You know him?"

"He's a friend of mine."

"And I'm first cousin to Alma Cogan!"

"Honest. We used to hang around together in his Stockport days. He comes from Stockport, did you know?"

She knew. He did.

"What time shall I be ready?"

"Pick you up at seven-thirty."

Donny replaced the receiver and went to clear out the back of his shooting brake. He hauled out the drums and spread a tartan blanket over the floor. It was not thick enough. He made the trip to his bedroom and came back with the eiderdown. He laid that on the floor and put the blanket on top of it, folding it over until he considered it to be fit for his purpose.

6

Sunday morning following that particular Friday found Ruth driving south in a pair of dark glasses, to alleviate a bit of a hangover. The Stonemason's had had a big party after their Saturday session. Even though Ruth had left before the end, she had indulged in more alcohol than was good for her. Enough to make her feel like signing the pledge the following day. She stopped at the first tobacconist's shop she found open and bought a box of good cigars and a birthday card. She had almost forgotten her father's birthday, and it came to her with that clarity that comes on waking, even with a hangover, that he was to be eighty years old today.

He might not be able to smoke the cigars, because he had been ill for some time. At his age he might even die soon, but she hoped he would be pleased to have them, whether he could smoke them or not. Pleased that she had remembered him.

She had not seen her parents much recently. Not since she had gone North with Sarah. Her mother had kept trying to persuade her to stay put and let Sarah work out her own problems. She kept inviting young men around in the hope that one of them might tempt Ruth into a relationship. They both knew what was happening, but Ruth did not want to argue about it. She simply refused to discuss it. So Mrs Anderton must have felt totally defeated when her daughter and Sarah had left together and disappeared into the back of beyond doing heavens knows what. Ruth's father, as always, trusted her to know what she was about, but they both probably worried about her. Most parents worry, after all. So it was only fair to let them see that she was still in the land of the living and to tell them about the TV programme before somebody else did.

They were hardly likely to see it themselves. Pop music was inclined to make her father switch it off at source and rush to the record cabinet for a healing dose of Palestrina. But they were sure to be told about it by others.

"Wasn't that your daughter with that strange group? What had she done to her hair?"

Then her parents would be upset because they had not known about it. She had balked at trying to bridge the generation abyss.

She began to sing as she sped down the motorway. The sun was shining. The countryside was green. Their stint at the Granary had been, if anything, even more successful last night than the one before. The popularity of the Stonemasons had grown so much that they were kept on for an extra hour, while being plied with liquid refreshment by the management. Afterwards they had been joined by the film crew for a farewell party which lasted into the small hours. The man in the camel-hair coat had been there. He was an agent called Robert Collinson who was going to take on the Stonemasons. From now on he would handle all publicity, bookings, recordings, TV appearances and possible tours. Life was opening out like a flower to the sun.

'Thank you, Lucy and Eileen, for saving me for this,' she thought. Her overdose had not been a cry for help. She had been thirsty for death. But since then her future had brightened up in more than one direction.

What a lovely morning! Her headache was now gone. She turned off from the motorway and into the leafy lanes of Warwickshire. The sun shone through the young leaves until they glowed like stained glass. It was God's annual promise: 'Behold, I shall make all things new!'

She was glad that she had avoided talking to her mother and father properly about Sarah. 'This is my life,' she would have said. For now Sarah was her life no longer and she would look as foolish as she felt. They would be pleased when she told them, as she would doubtless have to, because her mother would not leave the question unasked, that she and Sarah no longer saw one another. She would not go on to explain, however, the reason. It would be too painful to have to admit that Sarah belonged to her children; and that, when forced to choose, it was to her children that Sarah had returned. Ruth was not, could not be Sarah's life. She must carry on alone.

So she drove south to the parents to whom she did belong. The parents who were almost strangers. She wished that she had had brothers and sisters. She wished that she had not spent so much of her childhood being shipped off to boarding schools. She wished that her mother had been as easy to get on with as her father had always been. Some women could chat to their mothers as if they were friends. Could enjoy their company.

"What you need is a nice man."

She could hear her mother's voice as plainly as if she were there in the car. Why did nice men leave her cold? When did it happen?

Old stone walls went by and undulating fields lined with hawthorn hedges decked in blossom. Some of the villages still boasted the odd pond, complete with ducks. She passed the Norman arch of a church entrance, where people in smart clothes were shaking hands with the minister, as distinctive in his vestments as a magpie amongst starlings. In another couple of miles she would be rounding the bend that meant home. If only she could return as easily to that happy childhood state where love was innocent and there was no fearful truth about herself that had to be faced.

She looked at her watch. She would just be in time for lunch. Would they still have sherry before eating? Or was that another pleasure which he must now forgo?

She had expected to see Cheryl at the Granary last night. But the single-minded little drummer had not been there. Donny had turned up with a fat lip and a limp. He said he had been set upon by a jealous husband, but he kept glaring at her as though she was personally responsible. He had probably drunk too much and got into a brawl on the Friday evening.

Raggle Taggle must have been playing yesterday evening. All the same they finished at ten at the Black Cat. Cheryl could easily have come on to the Granary afterwards. She would suggest it to her on Wednesday when she saw her at band.

The band! Now that was something that would amuse her father. His daughter was taking the top cornet part in a women's brass band! She would turn the conversation in that direction as soon as she had told them about the group, so that they need not dwell on the pop music aspect. Maybe he would even be a little pleased. It was because of his love for the trumpet that she had taken it up as her second instrument; even though it was Bach and Purcell he adored, which was a world away from Regimental Selection.

She turned into the familiar drive and, lo and behold, it was full of cars! Many people must have considered this to be a special occasion, the eightieth birthday of Bishop Anderton. Feeling almost like an intruder, she found a space for her Hillman at the end of a long line of Bentleys, Daimlers and Rolls-Royces. She picked up her modest present and climbed out. She wished she had not come, but it was too late to go back now.

On Wednesday Lucy brought a large quantity of posters to the practice and insisted that everybody take at least one and find somewhere prominent to put it.

"Shops – pub doorways – stick them on your cars."

"We haven't got a car," came the inevitable objection from Rachel.

"Garden gate then, or your instrument case. There's always a way if you put your mind to it. And don't leave everything to one person. We must all pull our weight."

Annette approached her.

"I'm going to be away for six weeks. From the end of May."

"Six weeks? That's a long time!"

"It's training. For a job. I've been offered a job in beauty culture."

"Well I'm very pleased for you, Annette, but I hope you'll keep your lip in practice. You can soon lose your embouchure if you don't keep it going, so I'm told."

Annette had to smile at the idea of being allowed to practice the trumpet while on a course with fellow beauty culturalists.

"The thing is," she added, "when I get back, I'll be working in Manchester."

"Manchester!"

"That's right. I'll have my own car by then, I hope, but I don't know how easy it will be to continue coming to band."

Lucy was aghast and her face showed it.

"Tell me you're not going to leave us. Swear it in writing."

"I don't know. I can't tell yet. All I can say is that if I can come to band I will come to band. I do enjoy it, you know."

She turned away to avoid further argument on the subject. Ruth was not in the room. She would be outside having a smoke. Annette was about to join her as was her custom, when she hesitated. There was some tricky fingering she needed to sort out in one of the pieces so that it would not catch her unprepared as it had previously. Time was short. She must do it now.

Outside Ruth lit her cigarette and breathed a plume of smoke into the evening air. Every week the sky was a little lighter than the last. Life was improving at the same rate. She had seen many old faces at her father's birthday celebration. They had told her what they were doing and asked what she was doing and they told each other they hadn't changed a bit and wasn't it nice to see you! She had not really been as isolated as she had imagined.

She must go back home again some time soon.

Her cigarette was almost finished and Annette had not come for a chat. Not that she was obliged to. They had never made a special arrangement about it. She must have had something to discuss with somebody else. All the same, it made Ruth realise just how much she had come to look forward to her chats with Annette. It was not that she desired her physically. It was something to do with speaking the same language. That was rarer than sexual attraction. Maybe it was more important as well.

Ruth threw the remains of her cigarette into the long-suffering stream and returned inside.

Seeing that they were all there. Lucy ran through a list of stall-holders, with instructions for nobody to be late. She caught Annette's eye as she added that last bit.

Her little homily over with, Lucy took up the stick once more. They gave *Eventide* a run-through, did the tricky bits of *Blackrock Bay* and finished with *Regimental Selection,* in the course of which Cheryl at least could enjoy herself.

Afterwards, Ruth clicked her cornet case shut and went to help Cheryl with her drum kit, seeing as Annette was not, apparently, in a sociable mood today.

61

"Can I give you a hand?" she asked Cheryl's back. The drummer was occupied packing something away.

Strangely, she made no reply.

"They told us they were satisfied with the filming on Friday," Ruth persevered, choosing a subject which she was sure Cheryl could not ignore. "It's all gone to be edited. I'll let you know when they plan to screen it."

Cheryl turned round and looked her full in the face. Her eyes were like splintered glass.

"Don't bother," she spat. "I'm not interested."

Ruth took two paces backwards, feeling as if she had walked nose-first into a glass door.

"What's the matter?" she gasped when she could get her breath back.

"Just leave me alone, can't you?" Cheryl shot the words over her shoulder like a handful of stones. "That's not too much to ask, is it?"

"No," Ruth managed to utter. "That's not too much to ask."

She turned on her heel and took her battered feelings outside. If that was how Cheryl reacted when gently put in her place by Ricky, then she was certainly not worth bothering with. It was a sharp lesson not to go looking for more relationships. She would stay out of the kitchen. The heat was too much for her.

She took out her ignition key and opened the door of her Hillman, trying to think of a handy cliff she could drive over. Damn! Her cornet was still in the band room. She would wait until the Raggle Taggle van had been and gone before putting her head over the parapet again.

Desperate for privacy, she climbed in, almost catching the Jaguar alongside with her door. She put her head in her hands. Tears were fighting to come. She lit a cigarette. Her hands were shaking. She must get a grip on her feelings. Why did people have feelings? Feelings make fools of us all.

Someone tapped on her window. It was Annette. She was carrying two cases along with her handbag. Ruth wound down her window and she passed the cornet through.

"I told you she was obnoxious, didn't I. Come for a drink?"

Ruth felt too fragile to be seen in public.

"I must go home," she whispered. "But I'd welcome your company if you want to come to me for a drink."

Annette thought about it.

"I don't know where you live."

"Follow my car."

"All right, but don't go haring off like a hoodlum."

"I wouldn't dare, with a Jaguar on my tail."

"I like your house," Annette said later, as she stepped into the hall, accompanied by the dark shape of a cat who sometimes claimed Ruth as his provider. Doubtless some other householder was reporting him missing.

"Rented," Ruth told her. "I'm looking for somewhere smaller now. Know of anywhere?"

"I'll ask Harold. He dabbles in the property market."

"I love the word 'dabbles.'" Ruth said grimly. She poured two drinks and added a saucer of milk for the cat. "What would you like to listen to? Elgar, Ellington or Elvis?"

"What a choice! Have you got Bagpipe Favourites of 1908?"

"I've lent it out."

"Thank heavens for that."

Ruth bent down to open the record cabinet. While her face was hidden by the open double doors she said quietly, "Thanks for picking up my cornet."

"Yes. Well. I could see you were upset. What was wrong with Madame Krupa?"

"I have no idea."

Ruth emerged with an LP which she put on the turntable.

"What a bitch!" commented Annette, picking up her drink

63

and sinking into a chair. "That was my last practice for a while," she continued. "I'll be at the sale on Saturday. Then I'm off."

The deep brown sound of a cello filled the room with the strains of Elgar's *Chanson du Nuit*. Its melancholy could not have caught the tone of Ruth's feelings better.

"I shall miss you," she sighed.

"Not so many wrong notes."

"That as well, of course."

"Cheek!" Annette flopped back lazily in the chair, holding her glass in long pale fingers, listening to the soulful strings.

"Who's going to look after the children?" asked Ruth.

"Harold's mother. I think the kids are looking forward to having their grandma to stay. They get treats all the time."

"Won't you find it hard to leave your children?"

"Not for six weeks, I don't think."

"As long as it's only a short time."

"And they're not babies. Harold and I went to Norway when Tim was only five months old. I spent the whole fortnight phoning up to check he was all right. Drove everybody nuts."

Ruth stared unseeing at the record cabinet, thinking many things. Annette regarded her thin, intelligent face, her denimmed legs crossed like a man's, ankle over knee. She could see how a woman might find her sexy.

"Have you never been attracted to men?" she asked.

"No. Not properly."

"Why is that, do you think?"

Ruth put her glass to her lips, drained it and rose to get another.

"How the hell do I know?"

She delivered a kick to the waste paper basket. It flew across the room, scattering screwed-up manuscript, hit the door jamb before bouncing across the kitchen, bringing a startled cat skittering out with its ears down, fragments of topside in its wake. Thomas made a racing driver's turn out of the kitchen, claws scrabbling at the tiles as he fought against sideways drift, and leaped for the slightly-open window, flattening himself like toothpaste to squeeze through, his back legs working frantically.

Both women yelped with laughter, before kneeling on the floor to pick up the little bits of steak before they became trodden in. There was a pause from the record player. Then the happy strains of *Chanson du Matin* broke out, filling the room with audio sunshine.

"Sarah went back to her children," Ruth said suddenly, while their faces were turned downwards. "That's why she left me. They meant more to her than I did."

Annette sat up on her heels, holding meaty scraps in her palm.

"Where do I put these?"

"Give them to me."

Ruth made her add them to the collection in her own hand. It brought them close. She longed to fling her arms round that slender neck and bury her face in that soft feminine hair, but she held back. She valued too much the friendship which had recently blossomed between them, to risk throwing it away for the satisfaction of a fleeting physical desire.

Annette followed her into the kitchen, because she needed to wash her hands. She was not unaware of Ruth's feelings, nor entirely sure of her own. She picked up the tablet of soap and turned it round thoughtfully under the running tap.

"Perhaps it was herself she couldn't live with," she said at last. "I mean Sarah. It was herself, not you, that she couldn't live with. Have you ever thought of that? With children, you can't always please yourself. Not when they're tiny. You have to make a lot of sacrifices. You have to put yourself second."

Ruth threw her a towel.

"You're drying your hands on the curtains," she said.

7

The day of the Sale of Work arrived with startling rapidity. Ruth had given it little thought and as a result it crept up on her unawares. She had had to scrape around among her own resources for what books she could spare, before transporting them in the boot of her Hillman to the band room where it was to be held. Everything took place there. It was Rivington Church Hall and it housed the Sunday School as well as the Christmas pantomimes. It was home to wedding receptions, whist drives, bible readings and performances by the Amateur Dramatic Society.

It was a square stone building with a pitched roof covered in Welsh slate. A couple of side rooms flanked the entrance. One of these housed rows of hooks for coats. The other was used as a kitchen, where the women helpers stacked the piles of massive metal teapots ready for parties and other social occasions.

The large, echoing interior had a polished wooden floor for dancing on; the walls were painted that peculiar sickly shade of pale yellow which only seems to appear in public buildings. A stage at the far end was flanked by dressing rooms on each side, where chairs could be stacked when not needed.

She arrived soon after mid-day. Several cars were already taking up space in the road outside and a hum of voices could be heard coming from inside the building as Ruth opened the boot of her car and picked up a cardboard box-load of paper-backs, rehearsing a few apologies for the small amount of reading matter she had brought with her.

Lucy waylaid her as soon as she put her nose through the door.

"Did you bake us a cake?"

"Was I supposed to?"

"Oh well, perhaps not."

She could no longer remember whom she had or had not asked.

"Personally I wouldn't recommend one of my cakes," Ruth threw over her shoulder as she gazed around trying to spot a place in which to put down her cardboard box.

"I'm sure you're only saying that."

Luckily it was not to be put to the test. Instead, Eileen directed her to a trestle which had already been set up by obliging parishioners, who had piled it to wobbling point with books and magazines of all shapes and sizes, awaiting a sort-out.

Ruth need not have worried about the paucity of her own contribution; only about how she was going to cope with it all.

"Is there just me on this stall?" she asked, not knowing where to start.

"I've asked Susie to help you. She's collected a whole load of comics, is that all right?"

"Certainly. It's very welcome."

Somebody had placed a box of elastic bands on a corner of the trestle with which to secure rolled-up magazines. If there was time she could sort the comics into bundles of three or four and sell them like that.

"Can you send her over to help me do some sorting?"

"As soon as she arrives."

"Never mind, then," sighed Ruth.

Of course thirteen-year-old Susie, who was Eileen's daughter and played the E flat bass, arrived as soon as Ruth had finished dividing the works into fiction, biography, cookery, gardening etc and, once in her station, she made only half-hearted attempts to roll up the comics. She kept stopping to read them. She was not much use, but it was still better for Ruth than being stuck on a stall on her own.

Some of the stalls were immensely busy. As expected, the cakes were much sought-after. The toy counter was under siege and the many customers wanting flowers kept Annette and Judith busy wrapping and counting out change. The books did only a moderate trade, but always looked well patronised because many of the bored husbands and sons drifted over and stood around reading the time away, often without making a purchase.

"I'm going to charge you sixpence a minute," Ruth warned one particularly persistent offender and he put down the magazine and disappeared. Ruth found a novel by Evelyn Waugh which she had not read and also one by Virginia Woolf that she had always meant to tackle one day. She paid for them both and put them aside, then spent her time between customers sorting the hard-backs into alphabetical order.

Cheryl was managing the bric-a-brac stall on the other side of the room with the help of her family and, as far as Ruth was concerned, the further away the better. She had seen her directing her platoon in pinning up elephant-shaped white paper cut-outs before the place had filled up with people. Nothing would persuade her to get within spitting distance of that young woman again. She had to prove, if only to herself, that she had learned her lesson at last.

The sale, as is the way with these events, reached its busiest peak shortly after opening. From then on time passed quickly until, before they knew it, the density of bodies in the room began to thin out. Many people had drifted with their purchases to the tea area for refreshments. A cup of tea began to seem more and more like a good idea. She was just wondering whether she could leave Susie in charge while she went to get one when she saw Annette approaching with what seemed to be the same idea. She was wearing a brilliant white dress beside which everybody else appeared dowdy.

"Can Susie manage for a minute if you come with me?"

"I doubt it, but let's put her to the test. Where to?"

"Come and have your fortune told. Madame Zoro, alias Maggie Baxendale, is going to pick up her crystal ball and spirit herself away soon. She won't be here any more if we wait until we've cleared the produce and tidied up."

"You don't believe in all that rubbish do you?"

"Of course I do. Come on."

"Only if you treat me to a cup of tea afterwards."

"Good idea."

Later, when the sale had finished and everybody else had packed up and gone home, Ruth and Annette sat on the low wall by the stream, having a cigarette each. Harold had taken his sons to the rugby match and his wife would not be picked up until he had fought his way out through the crowd and driven through the heavy traffic all the way from Wigan.

"I can drive you home if you like," volunteered Ruth. She still had that melancholy feeling. It would not go away, because Annette was leaving for London and Paris and might never continue playing in the band.

"We could walk there if these shoes weren't beginning to cut into my feet. It's less than a mile."

"Won't Harold drive straight here? If we started walking we could miss him and he might spend ages circling around looking for you."

"I suppose he might. Anyway it's too hot," Annette told her. "Let's just sit here and chat and enjoy it. Unless I'm keeping you from your evening meal."

"I can get some chips on the way home. I'm not hungry."

"We'll not see one another again for a long time."

"I know."

Ruth blew a long lung full of smoke over the water. It was caught by the breeze and vanished almost at once. That should set the midges coughing.

"Cheer up," said Annette. The hunch of Ruth's shoulder and the droop of her arm told the whole story. "Didn't Madame Zoro say something about love on the horizon?"

"Yes," agreed Ruth. "That's part of her patter, isn't it. Tell the idiots what they want to hear." She drew on her cigarette and blew out some more smoke. "At least she didn't say a tall dark stranger. I give her that."

"A short fair acquaintance would have been more probable."

"No it wouldn't."

Annette sighed.

"I always said Cheryl was obnoxious."

"Yes. You just didn't say *how* obnoxious."

Annette cast away her cigarette only half smoked. She did not often smoke but she had accepted one from Ruth when it was offered. Unfortunately the wind was in just such a direction as to cause the smoke to keep drifting into her eyes. A screwed-up face was inelegant. She stretched out her legs and rotated her feet in ankle-slimming exercises.

"Madame Zoro told me I was going away and coming back," she mused. "I find that quite amazing."

"Not if she happened to know you were going on a training course."

"How would she know that?"

"Gossip gets everywhere," Ruth told her. "Believe me, gossip gets everywhere."

"Yes but then she told me something else. She said that if I go away a second time, I won't come back."

That was not something Ruth wished to hear.

"Well then you've been warned, haven't you. Don't go away twice."

"But if I don't go away a second time I'll never know if she was right or not."

"Exactly. Perfect nonsense, isn't it."

Ruth watched a butterfly dance past. Another one joined it and together the two cartwheeled and swooped together in mid-air courtship. They were Painted Ladies. It gave Ruth pleasure to watch them, eager as she always was to feel akin to nature, however unjustifiably.

"Did she give you any warnings?" Annette wanted to know, following her gaze but seeing only two anonymous butterflies. "Anything you can check on, to see if she's genuine?"

"She did, actually."

Ruth did not want to go on, but Annette was poised, still and silent, waiting to hear. Really she took these things far too seriously.

"She told me to beware success," Ruth divulged at last.

"Beware success?"

"Yes. How about that? Success can be dangerous, she told me. Everybody wants it, but watch out when it comes."

"She thinks you're going to have some success, then?"

"Seems like it. I felt like telling her to give me the success and I'll do the worrying. Let's see the colour of your success, I felt like saying."

"Do you think she'd seen you on the TV and recognised you?"

"Maybe." Ruth shifted her position and put both feet up and hugged her knees. "The Stonemasons have had a documentary done. We were filmed last week. It's one of a series."

"A series of what?"

71

"Programmes on unknown pop groups. Up and coming groups from all over the country, looking at what sort of music they play; what sort of people they are. They've done individual profiles, background, that sort of thing. We were chosen from the whole of the North West, on the strength of our performance at the pop festival in Manchester. They used my song as an example of our style of music." She threw the end of her cigarette into the stream and added, as much to herself as to her companion, "She can't have known about that, can she?"

"Mmmmmm. A bit creepy. But what marvellous news! Will I be able to see it, if I'm in London?"

"I think so. This is a nation-wide series. It'll be networked. I'll let you know the screening date if you write and give me your address."

"I'll write anyway. Tell you what a glorious time I'm having. Make you envy me for a change."

"You think I don't envy you already?"

"Why should you? House-bound housewife, with only the children's mumps and special offer price cuts to provide excitement."

"That's nonsense and you know it."

Annette caught a glimpse through the trees of the Jaguar passing the lower reservoir and knew it was only a couple of minutes away. She leaned close enough to deliver a brief kiss on the side of Ruth's face.

"That's to remember me by."

She jumped down quickly and dusted her skirt with her hand for any grime it may have picked up on the wall.

"Wait a minute. Arn't you going to let me return the compliment?" protested Ruth.

"Some other time. Sorry."

The Jaguar was coming and the last thing Annette wanted was for Harold to catch her in a clinch with Ruth.

A car load of children's high-pitched voices drew up and

Annette was received back into the bosom of her family. The car did a three-point turn, hands waved from its windows, then it accelerated away in a cloud of dust and Ruth was left alone. She turned away to where her own little Hillman waited for her, its fluffy octopus mascot that Sarah had given her dangling from the rear-view mirror. She rummaged in her handbag to locate the ignition keys, climbed aboard and drove back to the abode where Sarah would not be waiting for her.

Ruth had found a small flat on the wrong side of Chorley. She was to move in on Sunday and had begun the process of clearing out drawers and cupboards and stacking things up and packing things in containers. Thomas had not been back since the topside incident and her hallway was dreary as she picked her way through the obstacles, carrying hot chips wrapped in newspaper.

"Welcome to Anderton Hall," she greeted herself, as she passed a smokey mirror on her way to the kitchen. She put out a plate for the food and took a knife and fork from the drawer. She switched on the tape recorder to play the tape which had been made of her song, turning up the volume. Then she found a tin of Coke to wash down her chips.

Later on she would shower and change and join Ricky and the others at the Granary. She would be glad to get out and be amongst friends, who could keep her mind busy with the cut and thrust of entertaining a room full of the paying public, out to enjoy themselves. She wanted to lose the feeling of foreboding which hung around her like the hum of an engine which she could not switch off. She wished she had not gone to see Madame Zoro. Success had been all she had left to look forward to.

8

The following Wednesday Ruth picked up her cornet and took herself off to the band room for the practice as usual. The spirit of optimism hit her quite palpably as she walked through the door, cornet case in hand. Florence was her usual bouncy self, but Gladys was actually smiling at people and Alice could be heard to hum softly to herself. Judith was talkative. Teenage sisters Rachel and Rebecca were making themselves useful by putting chairs out for their elders. There was a general feeling that better things were within reach.

Moreover, there were three extra players. Cheryl had trawled through her friends and persuaded some of the brass-players of her old school to join Lucy's band. Once they were all seated and ready. Lucy announced the sum which had been raised. It drew a complete tonal range of "Eeee!"s from the assembly.

"You can trust me to make it go as far as I can," she told them, "and if there's any over, I'll give it to the church. Does everyone agree with that?"

Even Gladys raised no objection. So Lucy asked them to find *Eventide*. While they were busy putting up their well-thumbed copies of this on their music stands, Lucy, noticing that she now had only one top cornet, moved young Wendy up to the front bench next to Ruth. There was nothing too difficult in the piece for a child who showed promise and she could learn a good deal from working with a skilled player. Then Lucy gave them the downbeat and they burst into sound.

The piece was well-chosen. Its slow pulse and sustained notes demanded a mellow tone. So it was better without the brilliant timbre of Annette's trumpet. In that respect at least she was not missed.

But her absence was felt by Ruth. When she went outside at the break time nobody came to chat with her. She had already received a post card from London, with a picture of the statue of Sir Winston Churchill and the words 'I shall return' scrawled below it. Annette must have got him confused with De Gaulle. The reverse side was covered by an excited chatty scribble that extended to all the spaces round the print and was hard to decipher.

Ruth put out her cigarette and returned to her seat, where she passed the rest of the break giving her mouthpiece a brushing-out which it did not really need. She was in good lip this evening. So when they came to the cadenza in *A Medley of Scottish Airs*, she decided to give it the works. She built up the suspense with a slow, quiet start, gave a few tentative runs, hovering like a diver on the edge of the board, keeping them guessing then she rushed up to the top with incredible speed, hung onto her top D with a singing tone that faded to an almost impossible pianissimo. There was a sliver of silence, before she made a descent as exhilarating as a ski run, accelerating into the cheering crowd at the finishing line, which was what the band sounded like as it joined her in triumphant forte. Lucy had never heard her play so well before. She was never to hear her play so well again.

Afterwards she stopped Ruth as she was leaving.

"That was a right gradely effort in Scottish Airs."

"All part of the service, Lucy. The lip service, if you like."

Lucy gave a brief smile to acknowledge the joke, before getting down to business.

"Are you free any morning this week?"

"Friday."

"I'll pick you up at ten, all right? We'll go to Wythenshaw."

"Fine."

Friday brought the kind of weather for which Manchester is famous. It rained lavishly for long enough to give everything a proper wash, but it had eased off to a mere spatter by the time Lucy and Ruth came out of the Music Exchange, laden with reams. Tall buildings dripped, down-pipes gushed. Stepping near the edge of a pavement was a bit like walking on a jetty at high tide. But the sun came through a cloud and suddenly it was early summer again.

"I'm gasping for a cup of tea," said Lucy. "Have you got time for one?"

"You bet."

Ruth would have liked something stronger, but then, she was not doing the driving. They left the music in Lucy's car and took a bus into the city centre. Lucy knew exactly where she was heading, being a bit of a tea buff. She guided Ruth to a little specialist cafe off Deansgate where all the tables had spotless white cloths with lace edging and the waitresses wore white caps and pinnies. The two settled into their chairs with the kind of groans women give when their feet are tired of their shoes.

"I see there's a recital on at the Free Trade Hall," observed Ruth, reading a poster on the door, after they had given their order and were waiting for the results to appear. A help-yourself cafe at the bus station would have suited her fine. She stretched out her legs and spun her much-too-striking unisex hat onto a spare chair. Lucy longed to tell her sharply to act a bit more lady-like.

"Schubert and Ravel," Ruth continued.

"Piano recital is it?" asked Lucy, hunting for her long-distance glasses. "Pity we can't go. I've offered to pick up my neice's little daughter this afternoon.

"That's very kind of you."

"It's no bother for me. She's a single mother."

"Intended? Or accidental?"

There was a bit of a pause before Lucy added, "Someone spiked her drink at a party. She didn't know anything about it until months later."

"Oh no. How awful!"

A pot of tea was delivered to them on a tray, with a couple of delicate china cups, a jug of hot water and a plate of tiny petit fours.

"And she decided to keep the baby," Ruth continued. "That was brave of her."

"Of course she did," replied Lucy in a tone which should have warned Ruth to keep off the subject. But it had been eating away at Ruth's heart since Sarah left and she could not leave it alone.

"I admire her attitude. To care for the child. You know —"

Lucy put down her cup. Some straight talking was needed

"You may not understand this, Ruth, but bringing up a child is a privilege. Children are the most important thing in this world." She dabbed the tea bag up and down in the pot a little. The tea was on the weak side. "They may take up all your time and your patience... and your money, come to that. They may worry you, they may hurt you. They will certainly keep you awake at night.

"But it doesn't matter. Because of what they give you in return. It's hard to tot it up on a piece of paper. It's not what you call quantifiable. But they can bring out things in your character that you never knew were there. They can teach you so much."

"Give you a purpose in life?"

"Oh definitely! They definitely give you a purpose in life.

And they bring out the best kind of love; the unselfish kind; the kind that wants to give and not to take."

She selected a couple of petit fours and transferred them to her plate.

"You have to make sacrifices…" began Ruth, but Lucy was in full flood now and was not to be stemmed.

"Sacrifices? Of course you make sacrifices. Sacrifices that are not really sacrifices. A child will take from you all the things that don't matter and give to you all the things that do." She put a morsel into her mouth and sipped her tea and continued with hardly a break. "And it doesn't matter where it comes from or how it is conceived, or even whether it is sound in body and mind. A child is the greatest blessing you could have in this life. Another cup?"

The tea was darker now.

"No thanks, Lucy."

Ruth picked up a petit four which she did not really want. She felt very depressed. Lucy saw her expression and moderated her tone. Her companion was not a bad person. It must be a lonely kind of life, the one she had chosen for herself.

"Why don't you find yourself a nice man, Ruth? Have some children of your own. Then you would know."

"Sounds easy, doesn't it."

"It shouldn't be too difficult, for an attractive girl like you. Talented, too. You've got such a lot to offer."

"But not love. Isn't that important?"

"There's more than one kind of love in this life, and some of them are worth working at. You'll realise the truth of that as you get older."

Ruth picked up her hat and turned it round in her hands.

"Lucy, that fortune-teller at the sale. Is she genuine?"

"Did she say you were going to meet a tall dark stranger?"

"If she'd said that I wouldn't be asking you if she were genuine."

"I've heard people say she's uncanny. I've never been to her myself. I believe that if you take care of the present the future will look after itself."

"The things she's told people. Do they come true?"

"So they say." Lucy fetched her tongue round her mouth in search of stray crumbs and made a sign to the waitress. "People have said so. Of course you can apply them to what's going to happen anyway. You know what I mean. 'Bad News by Post!' Then the electricity bill arrives."

"Exactly. It's so vague, isn't it. 'Danger in success'. That could mean getting an awkward tin of corned beef open, then cutting your finger on the lid."

"Is that what she told you? Danger in success? She told one of our WI members not to go out in the snow. Molly had a good laugh because we all thought winter was over. It was the end of March. Lovely sunshine at the time. Then we had that blizzard in April and she fell down the steps and broke her leg."

"Oh!"

Ruth wished she had never set eyes on Maggie Baxendale. She also wished Lucy would hurry up and finish picking around with what was basically miniature food and tea that tasted of nothing so much as the water that you'd cooked things in.

Then the waitress arrived and Lucy insisted on paying the bill and Ruth did not argue the matter and they made their way back to the station for the Wythenshaw bus.

On the way there they walked past one of the few remaining areas that was still waiting to be built upon after having been flattened during the war. The site was cleared and several cars were perched between large stretches of puddle.

"It looks as though you could have driven right into the centre and parked here."

"Yes but we weren't to know that were we? There was fencing around it last time I was here. Someone must be going to develop it at last."

They turned the corner and glimpsed across the road the bright blue doorway of a night club with the words *The Sapphire* over the top. Ruth hesitated. Where had she heard that name? Then she remembered Muriel Helpman and her little card. She wanted to cross the road and take a closer look. But Lucy was rushing ahead, so Ruth hurried after her.

The practice on the following Wednesday should have been one of the most enjoyable, with the new pieces they had bought. There was a selection of Nat King Cole favourites and some Guy Mitchell numbers which should have put *Regimental Selection* into permanent retreat. There was also a note-packed piece called *Capriccio* with a virtuoso cornet part that was quite easy for the rest of the band if Ruth took the solo.

But the Guy Mitchell turned out to be rather a problem for the horn section, who did not constitute the band's strongest suit. They were not helped by the fact that the strongest player in that quarter, Mary on euphonium, was at home nursing her son who had 'flu. The soprano cornet was sharp again having, presumably, pushed her tuning slide back in again. Though Lucy made her adjust it, she never quite got into pitch, which made the whole band uncomfortable with their notes, since the ear tends to be guided from the top.

At break time Ruth went outside and puffed cigarette smoke at a cloud of midges. She was not enjoying herself. Here they were with some good music to get their teeth into and one player could send the whole band out of kilter. It was Lucy's problem, of course.

Annette had not written since that first post card. Why should she? She must have far more interesting things to do.

Ruth returned for the second half and they blew on until she cracked a top note. That, for her, was the end. If there was one thing she could not tolerate in herself it was cracking notes. She rose before the final march.

"I've got a splitting headache," she announced to Lucy. "Do you mind if I go?"

She drove out of the car park. Suicidal thoughts began to collect on the outskirts of her consciousness. Nobody wanted her. She was no use to anyone. She could not even play the cornet properly any more. She was a total failure as a human being.

But by the time she drew up outside her new residence she had got around to reminding herself firmly that the Stonemasons were shortly to appear on TV. She must stay alive at least for long enough to watch it.

She unlocked the front door and trudged up the dismal stairs to her horrid little flat. She filled the kettle and plugged it in. A spider scuttled in terror back into one of the food cupboards. A couple of woodlice were making a long trek to nowhere over the lino. She felt in her handbag for her cigarettes and out with them came a card. *The Sapphire*, it read, in bright blue letters. Underneath was printed the name and phone number of Muriel Helpman.

The noise of the kettle grew and grew in the small space. She flicked the card onto the work surface and when she had made a coffee she sat and smoked and stared at it as it lay there.

9

It was strange, seeing herself on a television screen. It looked like the sort of performance put on by somebody else, as though it were not really herself capering around like that. Ruth sat alone in her lounge watching it. She had chosen to do so that way. It was better to be alone if it made her cringe, as indeed some of it did.

"Oh no!" she moaned to herself. "Why didn't I check my hair from the back?"

"Tell me that isn't me!" she cried to a non-existent companion as the figure hooked the microphone back onto its stand and snatched up a trumpet, bringing it to the lips with a sweeping movement of the arm for all the world as though she were going to drink from a Spanish wine skin.

'What a poser!' she thought. What would Sarah think of her? If she were watching. Would she phone if she saw it, to congratulate or to have a laugh?

She must not think of Sarah. She concentrated on watching the screen. It seemed to her that the others, at any rate, were looking like the real thing. There was a close-up of Ricky's hands every time he did the glissando. Donny had got himself an outrageous coiffure for the occasion. His hair was sticking out all over the place while he attacked his kit as though he were trying to beat out some kind of fire. Of course the teeny-boppers loved it, clustering close to get into camera range. There were shots of their hysterical faces after every percussive flurry.

Ron had the good looks. He carried his head sullenly and proudly, as fashion demanded, and a dark sausage of hair fell over one eyebrow. You would never guess what an ineffectual kind of bloke he was in company.

She had to admire what the cameras did to them. The angles, the zoom-ins that centred on Donny's hammered-out quavers between the vocal lines, the backlit shots, the double exposures, the soft focus. That was where most of the professionalism lay; in the camera work.

Why did the telephone not ring? Ruth would have rushed to pick up the receiver. She would have heard that voice, as familiar to her as her own. They would have laughed together, always knowing what the other person was going to say even as she said it. Or so it had seemed to Ruth. But had it been the same for Sarah? Can she ever have really cared at all, to maintain such a silence now? How could she watch this programme and not get in touch?

Ruth cut off her own thoughts with a mental cleaver. She must prove to herself that she could be just as callous as Sarah was.

The music sessions were interspersed with interviews in which the performers were featured in turn and then all together. The boys gave plenty of background information. Their humble origins; their youthful exploits. Any unusual details, such as the pet squirrel that Ron, as a boy, had kept in the back shed, were seized upon by those whose job it was to make the program as entertaining as possible. Ruth, conscious of this, was glad that Donny did not know her true origins. She did not want to embarrass her father by having his bishophood bandied around as if it were an aberration. She informed the interviewer of the extent of her training in classical music, starting with details of her early piano lessons. She put on the most flat and monotonous voice she could muster and, as she had intended, he rapidly lost interest.

Donny knew how to play up to the occasion. He dreamed up an elaborate story of how *Going Down* came to be written, exaggerating the part the group had played in it and mercifully leaving out any reference to a suicide attempt. His version would doubtless help sell more singles, so she did not protest at the minor role attributed to her.

The phone had not rung. Of course it wouldn't. In all probability Sarah had not let herself watch the programme, even if she had been allowed to do so. It was part of the deal. No further contact with her lesbian lover. That was the condition for being taken back and reunited with her children. It did not mean that Sarah was not missing her. It did not mean that she was not suffering too. But their life together was over. They had to accept that.

Ruth switched off her TV and began to put her things together. The Stonemasons were playing at the Granary this particular evening. Friday nights, when they did them, were usually on the quiet side but tonight might be different, if many others had seen the programe too. It was the kind of publicity money could not buy. She ought to get there early in case people began to queue.

They did. Early as she was, there was a long line of people standing patiently outside the main door by the time her Hillman turned into the pockmarked car park. She had to push through serried ranks of humanity in order to get to the entrance, laden as she was with trumpet and guitar in their cases. There was an excited murmur as she did so. It was all rather unreal.

Donny and Ricky were already there, setting up the equipment on stage.

"Here comes the incredible female yo-yo," called Donny when he saw her.

"What about you?" she countered, "the unbelievable drumming hedgehog."

Ricky laughed, twanging the strings of his bass guitar and twirling knobs to test for volume. He was pleased with the effect his glissando had made. Ruth began to unpack her instruments.

"Ron not here yet?"

But even as she spoke there was a commotion at the door and Ron burst through, helped by the burly door man. He was dishevelled and lacking his tie.

"They're like mad dogs out there," he gasped. "And I must say, Ruth, the girls are the worst."

"Get set up," Donny told him. "Then we'll go and have a beer while the place fills up. I want some of those mad bitches after me."

The proprietor was actually rubbing his hands as he greeted them and ushered them to the bar for some free drinks. For they were about to make his fortune for him.

"Have a quick one now," he said, "and I'll make sure there's some champagne waiting for you in the side room for the interval. I'm expecting you to knock 'em dead."

He meant knock 'em wild, because that is what they did to their audience. There was a great cheer when they climbed onto the dais. The enthusiasm hit the group like a shot of cocaine. They plugged in, switched on, blew into mikes and launched straight into *Going Down*, though it is doubtful that much of it was heard, owing to the racket from the floor. Carried on the wings of the fans, they rose to heights beyond those they could normally attain. Lifted on the adrenaline of others, they gave a performance of unprecedented vitality. Their rhythm was tighter, their timing was slicker, they could not put a beat wrong. The Granary was packed from corner to corner and the fans were in raptures. If this was not success, then it would have to do.

"I think we're going to find out what it's like to be mobbed," yelled Ricky, not knowing whether to be scared or thrilled, as they battled their way towards the side room at the interval. The proprietor arranged for the door to be closed behind them and guarded and it was just as well. Suddenly privacy had become precious. They helped themselves from a tray of glasses into which a waiter was pouring champagne, though they were half inebriated already with the headiness of it all.

"Success can be dangerous all right," Ruth said to herself as she tried to slake a raging thirst on a mouthful of bubbles. "But I like it."

"Don't forget to give our album a plug," Ricky reminded Ron.

"Yeah," agreed Donny. "Memories are short and overdrafts are long."

"If they all buy one we'll be rich overnight," speculated Ruth.

"Is your little blue-eyed friend here tonight?" Ron wanted to know. "Ask her in. I really fancy her."

"She's not my little blue-eyed friend, thank you. And if she were I wouldn't let her into your clutches, believe me."

"Oh yah yah. Not got her going yet, then!" Ron gave a burst of disbelieving laughter. "Give over. You passed her on to Donny and he's worse than me."

"Of course I didn't. I wouldn't pass on a dead dog to Donny."

"That's not what I heard," said Ron, with a guffaw.

Ruth froze, her glass halted half-way to her mouth.

"Shut your face Ron," Donny came in quickly, seeing where the conversation was leading.

"No." Ruth's voice had an edge to it. "Don't shut your face Ron. Tell me all about Donny and my blue-eyed little friend."

"Why don't we leave it until another time?" Ricky plunged in brightly. "There's a crowd outside asking for autographs. Who's going first?"

"Nobody!" snapped Ruth, standing between the boys and the door. "Until you've told me what happened."

"I hope you're not going to be a silly hysterical female," complained Donny. "I took her out. Sorry to upset you. Was she yours?"

"What did you say to her?"

"I warned her off, if you want to know. She was getting to be a nuisance, hanging around when we were filming."

"So what did you say?"

"Maybe I just told her that one woman around is enough. Which it is. *More* than enough."

"You must have said more than that."

"Why?" Donny's eyes glittered. "What happened? Did you try to get her to bed? What did she do? Slap your face? I wish I'd been there." He hooted with rather forced laughter. "If you could see your face, Anderton!"

Ricky could see her face. He did not like what he saw. He put his arm around her shoulders.

"Don't take any notice," he told her. "He's the one who got clobbered. He got a bit more than his face slapped. He's just trying to save his pride."

Ruth shook off Ricky's arm, wishing she could stop trembling. It should not have mattered this much. But it did.

"Yes," she got out, running a tongue over her dry lips, "but what did you *say*, Donny?"

"He told her that you and he had a special arrangement," Ron divulged with a smirk, "You taught the girls a thing or two until they were drooling for it. then passed them on to him, if you know what I mean."

Donny thumped Ron in the side, causing him to spill champagne all over himself.

"Can't you shut your stupid shit-hole?"

"He was only trying to save his pride," cried Ricky, desperate to redeem the situation, "Donny was just trying to save his pride."

But Ruth had gone white.

"You sod! I'll kill you."

She threw the champagne at his head, still in the glass, and walked blindly out of the room. She felt sickened and demeaned. She saw none of the autograph hunters, nor any of the many people who stood between her and the Ladies'. She walked right through them. But there was going to be danger in success all right. For Donny.

"Let her go," said Donny, licking his hand, which had caught the glass and with it most of the champagne. "She had it coming."

But Ricky dived into the crowd after her.

"Two of a kind!" Donny sneered at his departing back. He raised his voice. "She's in the little girls' room, Ricky. You'll feel at home there."

The second stint was late in starting, what with cooling tempers and autograph hunters and Ricky trying to pull things back from the brink.

"Don't worry about Cheryl," he told Ruth when she at last emerged from territory where he could not go, whatever Donny's views on the matter. "I'll speak to her. I'll put it right for you." He had to shout it into her ear from behind as she strode back to the main hall, stopping to sign the odd program, but not paying him any attention.

"You won't do anything silly, will you, Ruth?" he caught her arm to force her to listen to him. "This is too important. Can you hear me? I'll tell Cheryl the facts."

But Ruth would not look at his face.

"Thanks, Ricky. You're a nice guy. Others are not."

She shook off his hand and climbed onto the stage.

So they started again, but their playing had gone off the boil. The spirit of unanimity had departed. Before long little things began to happen. Twice Donny slashed at his large cymbal just as Ruth, backing up to it, tilted it out of his reach, making him look remarkably foolish as he hit the silent air. On one occasion, she managed to flick her lead so that it whisked the stick out of his hand and he had to dive to the floor to retrieve it. He swore at her. His eyes were like pits.

"What's the matter, laughing boy?" she taunted him. "You're not laughing any more."

"Neither will you tomorrow," he snarled.

He stepped up his drumming to drown out her best vocal lines and she responded by fronting with trumpet what should have been his solo.

Much later, when the final encore was taken, the last fan persuaded to leave and they were packing away with a weary sense of achievement gone sour, she found that he had put his sticks on her trumpet case. Her inner anger burst out and she hurled them towards him across the floor.

It was just bad luck that he was stepping backwards at the time with the large cymbal in his hands, so that he trod on them, skidded, caught his foot in some flex and sat on the bass drum, breaking the skin. The cymbal came down on his face, cutting him above the eye.

"You shouldn't have done that, Ruth."

Ricky was the first to speak.

"It's hardly my fault if he's got feet like a camel and doesn't look where he's putting them."

Donny sat up and dabbed at the blood over his eye. Ron and the door man helped him to stand, while Ricky and Ruth waited for the storm which they were sure would be unleashed.

But there was no storm. Donny did not break her guitar over her head, or hurl anything heavy at her. He quietly got his things together and left them stacked in a corner, ready for Saturday's stint. Then still holding a hanky to his head and accepting the doorman's supporting arm, he walked to the exit, followed by Ron.

"Ten quid says she meets some naughty boys on the way home."

Donny spoke very quietly, slipping two fivers into the man's pocket. Then he turned and called out.

"Drinks at my place, Ricky? See you there."

"You bet," cried Ricky in relief.

But he did not ask Ruth.

"Come along in half an hour," Ricky suggested. "He'll have had time to simmer down by then."

"I wouldn't dream of it," she said. "I'm surprised you want to go. He's just a slimy, disgusting little rat."

But Ricky was not going to miss the big celebration with the lads in his hour of triumph. He was human, after all. So they all drove away and left her, alone in the car park.

The night was full of the insubstantial darkness that occurs around midnight in June. It was as quiet as velvet after the rumpus of the last few hours. Even the door man had disappeared on some errand of his own. Ruth threw her trumpet and guitar onto the back seat of her car. She climbed in, slammed the door and started the engine. It sounded subdued. Was she going deaf?

A feeling of flatness overcame her. Excitement had gone as if it had never been. She thought of the shabby little place in downtown Chorley that was now her home and felt a great disinclination to go back there. It was late. It was bed time. But she could not just simply go to bed.

As the car bumped down the long track towards Rivington Lane she thought of Annette and wished she was still around. She touched her cheek where that kiss had been placed with tantalising swiftness. It was the comfort of a fellow female that she needed right now. But it was nowhere to be found.

Or was it?

The car wheels forsook the gritty track for the smooth tarmac of the road and she headed not right for Chorley, but left for Manchester.

Why not the *Sapphire*? After all, places like that were intended for people like herself. Where else had she to go? Where else did she belong? It was only because of her upbringing that she recoiled from the idea as sordid.

But was it sordid, the search of the lonely for love and companionship? What could be wrong with that?

Not the same as Sarah. That's what was wrong with that. The difference between a love that came to greet you from a clear blue sky and the seeking out of a quick physical gratification. The two were not the same, or she would not have hesitated over Annette.

She was by now in Horwich, where she turned onto the new road to Bolton, with its sodium lights and its special surface that invited speed. It led to the ring road she would take for Manchester. She was too absorbed in her thoughts to notice that some headlights behind her turned the same way.

She was thinking about a little girl who had sat beside her mother in the front pews of a great cathedral and listened to the breathtaking beauty of treble voices echoing around the high stone fan-vaulted ceiling. She had vowed then to God that music would be her life. She thought of the Stonemasons and the noisy Granary and felt desperately sad. Life is so straightforward when you are eight years old.

It must have been midnight by the time she reached the city centre and found the old bomb site which she and Lucy had discovered too late to park on the other week. Her spirits were sinking and she was scared inside. But could she come this far and then turn around and go all the way back? She felt very alone. But all was not completely quiet. Another car was turning in.

Perhaps the *Sapphire* was closed by now. She would leave her trumpet in the car and just go along and see if it was open. It was a night club, after all. It would not be far to come back to retrieve the instrument if she was required to play. She climbed out and locked her car.

The streets were quiet, but not quiet enough, for the characters who hung around looked as seedy as the hour.

She reached the club and ducked into the foyer. The lights were dim and there was music coming from below. One or two erotic pictures involving females decorated the wall. They looked like a man's idea of what would excite a woman who preferred women. Somewhere in her handbag was Muriel Helpman's card. 'Just mention my name,' she had said. Would it work?

She was still getting her bearings when a couple came tottering up the stairs towards her from the dance room below. Although one was dressed in a suit, it was plain that they were both women. They were giggling like people who have had too much of something intoxicating. They stopped close to her and gave each other a passionate, open-mouthed kiss. The one in the suit opened one eye to assess Ruth over her partner's shoulder. Then they both fell over, hooting with silly laughter.

"We're pissed," one of them told her, confidentially.

Ruth told herself it was time to go.

"Get the hell out of here!" yelled a voice from an alcove, making her jump. "If you can't behave yourselves just leave the premises."

The passionate couple promptly tumbled back down the steps, still laughing. Ruth saw that there was a table in the alcove, where a door person sat by a money box and a pile of tickets.

"Is it always like this?"

The door person pulled a face.

"Are you looking for somebody in particular?"

"I – er – Ruth began fumbling in her bag."

"Are you a member?"

"No," said Ruth. Her fingers found the card. She handed it over. "I play the trumpet. Muriel Helpman told me I could drop in and play any time."

"You haven't got one with you?"

"It's in my car. Shall I get it?"

"Yes if you like. I'll send someone to check with the band."

Ruth went outside into the heavy night. The words of Madame Zoro came back to her like a bad dream. She had to remind herself that she did not believe in all that nonsense.

She crossed the road and had reached the corner when a nervous glance over her shoulder revealed a hulk of dark shadow, many-headed, many-footed, bobbing silently behind her.

"She doesn't like us, lads," came a voice.

"She's a lezzie, that's why."

Ruth hurried her step.

"She doesn't like men."

"Why doesn't she like men?"

"Perhaps she doesn't know what she's missing."

The amorphous mass was getting closer. Somebody hawked loudly and spat on the pavement.

"I bet she never had a good screw in her life."

"Somebody ought to do her a favour."

"Want to come here, darlin'? Got something to show you."

She arrived at the edge of the building site and it was horribly empty, but so were the streets ahead of her. If she reached the car she could at least lock herself in and sound the horn or something. It was only a few yards.

Clutching the key in her hand, she broke into a run and of course it was the signal for them to close in on her. They brought her down in the middle of the bomb site. It was about as deserted a spot as you could find in a living, breathing city.

Then they were all over her.

10

When Lucy arrived at the infirmary the next afternoon, she found Ruth conscious, but unable to speak. She was not going to be able to speak for some time. She was hardly recognisable. The lower half of her face was hidden by bandages and plaster, through which a hole only just large enough for a feeding tube to pass through had been made. The hair around her face had been shaved off and the rest cropped very short. Her eyes were bruised. She lay motionless and only sometimes fixing Lucy with her swollen eyes. When Ruth saw the horror in Lucy's face it made her feel worse than ever. She closed her eyes until her visitor had left.

Lucy found the staff nurse, who could only tell her that the patient had a badly broken jaw and a suspected fracture of the right fibula.

"Will she be all right?"

"I can't say. If you want to know more you'll have to ask the surgeon. You might just catch him if he hasn't left yet," she volunteered. "Down the corridor, turn left, up the stairs and first door on the right. Knock first," she flung over her shoulder as she padded off on her busy way.

Fortune was on Lucy's side. He was just changing into his

jacket and allowed her to fire questions at him as he made off towards his car and the Sunday game of golf which he still hoped to salvage. He was not keen to discuss a rape case, which could mean trouble and testimony in the future.

"Is she going to be able to play the trumpet again?" Lucy wanted to know.

"That I cannot say," he told her. "I've always been too busy to indulge in such recreational pursuits, however much I may have liked to. All I can say is that if she plays the trumpet again it will not be with quite the same jaw she played it with before."

"You mean she will have to re-learn?"

"Probably."

Arriving at his car, he brought a handful of keys from his pocket and sorted through them for the right one. Seeing her glum face, he smiled at her.

"Cheer up. She should be able to eat and speak, which are more important, I 'm sure you'll agree. She's lucky. It was quite a mess."

He climbed in and drove away, whistling cheerfully at the thought of the eighteen holes which awaited him.

Ruth lay immobile, shocked and in pain. Why hadn't Lucy let her die that time when she overdosed? She would have slipped away into the next life quite peacefully and this would never have happened to her.

Fuzzy with drugs, she drifted off to sleep again. She dreamed that she was on a beach and there were rocks... rocks of unearthly blue, black and red. The sea was indigo and emerald green. Its surface sparkled as though sprinkled with sequins. She was very thirsty and hot and her face hurt.

She noticed a child who was running around on the sand in bare feet. It found a shallow puddle nearby and stamped its feet up and down to splash water at her, gurgling with laughter. It turned its face with dark eyes towards her and raised little arms to be picked up. Filled with the kind of happiness that only comes in dreams, she reached out to it.

But then she was lying on something hard and flat. The child was gone and with it the sun. Darkness began to close in until she could hardly see. She was strapped to the ground, pinned there by a heavy object that was crushing her face, so that she could not move. The tears ran down the side of her face and into her ears.

She could hear the child crying, but she could not see it. It wanted her and she could not reach it. Her limbs were pinned down and she was helpless to to save it. She could not push away the heavy object and free herself. The crying became desperate. It grew fainter and fainter. It was being taken where she could not follow. It was suffering and she could not comfort it. A desolation swept over her, as if something precious were becoming irretrievably lost, left to cry alone in the coldness and the blackness. She woke to the sound of her own moans. Other heads in the ward were turned towards her. A nurse hurried up with a syringe and gave her an injection to ease the pain.

Ricky looked white and drawn when he saw her.

"What have they done to you?" he gasped. Foolish question. She could not answer and in any case what they had done was plain to see. He laid his sad little bunch of flowers on her bedside locker and she took his hand with one of hers and squeezed it, hoping he would take it as a mark of her gratitude for his concern. He told her that he wished he had not gone to the celebration. That he should have stayed and kept her company. That in any case the party was spoiled by the bad feeling which had been engendered, so he had left early. He needed to get that off his chest, hoping for her forgiveness, hoping it might make both of them feel better. Instead he felt more wretched.

What he could not tell her was that Donny had spent the celebration complaining about 'that Anderton dike' until they were all sick of him. There was a bloke he knew, he had said, with a tenor saxophone who could also manage a bit of keyboarding. He was all ready and waiting to drop into her shoes, Donny had told them. He was having no more bleeding females in his group, he said.

Well so it had turned out. Ruth could no longer be part of the Stonemasons.

The Wednesday band practice was a sad affair. Lucy had been unable to summon her emergency first cornets Joan and Deidre. The two had been friends since childhood and did everything together. It seemed this also included the timing of their pregnancies, because Joan had just given birth to her third baby and Deidre was due to follow suit any time soon. They both promised to come along as soon as they were ready, but for the present it was inconvenient.

If it had not been for the three new players whom Cheryl had recently recruited from the ranks of her contemporaries, Lucy would have had to cancel the fete and even disband. But luckily, one of them was a useful cornet player called Jo. So, with Annette absent, young Wendy and Jo had to hold down the top line with some support from Judith who sat behind them with the repiano part. Rebecca was the only lower cornet. In this way they could carry on rehearsals without the more adventurous part of their repertoire, which had to be left to moulder in the dust while they stuck to hymns and easy pieces.

After an uninspiring practice, therefore, Cheryl dropped off Sally and her bass as usual and drove home. She turned into her drive, switched off the ignition, opened the door and stepped out. As she did so a figure approached from the shadow. She quickly jumped back in and shut the door, locking it from the inside. The figure tapped on the window and pushed his face close so that she could see him. She recognised the bass player from the Stonemasons and slid the window back ever so slightly.

"What do you want?"

"Can I talk to you?"

"I've got my hand on the horn and I warn you it's very loud."

"There's no need for that. I've got something to say."

"Phone me. Phone me tomorrow."

"People can hang up on the phone," he pointed out. "I called at your house," he added, "But they told me you were at band practice. I thought I'd wait."

No girl could be frightened of Ricky for long.

"All right. Get in the other side. But you'd better behave yourself. Nobody tries anything on me more than once."

"So I gather."

He walked round the bonnet so that she could see him and climbed in the other side.

"I went to see Ruth in hospital," he began, giving her an enquiring glance to see her reaction, hoping she would respond.

But Cheryl did not reply. Her face was stony.

"I think a visit from you might do her a power of good."

"I'm not going to visit her. If that's what you came for you can go now."

She had been made to feel utterly cheap by Donny's suggestion, and that was hard for a Prescott-Withers to forgive.

Ricky sighed. He could not make her go. But he could still try to put her in the true picture.

"I think it's a pity that you were so easily taken in by Donny." he began. "I'd have expected someone of your intelligence to see what he was up to."

Cheryl turned her head to look at him then quickly looked away again.

"He sees you as a threat, you know." persevered Ricky. "As a drummer, I mean. I'm surprised it isn't obvious. You and Ruth together! What a team! Who needs Donny Mason?"

98

He paused, but Cheryl said nothing.

"He wanted to break up the two of you. He set out to make trouble between you and Ruth. Sadly, you swallowed the bait," he added.

He looked searchingly at Cheryl's pursed lips and set jaw, but still she threw him no line. He shrugged and put his hand on the door handle.

"You seem to have made up your mind, so I suppose it's no use trying to give you the rest of the story. Do you want it?"

When there was no reply he opened the door, ready to jump out. Cheryl watched him. For a couple of seconds it was bluff and counter-bluff. Then Cheryl spoke.

"Okay. Let's hear what you've got to say, then."

So Ricky pulled the door shut and told her about the best-ever gig, which had been spoiled by Donny and Ron, who started taunting Ruth about the 'no-show' of her 'little blue-eyed friend'. He described how sickened Ruth had been when Ron had let slip the exact nature of the lie which Donny had used to poison any potential alliance between the two girls. He told her how the bad feeling had escalated throughout the Stonemasons' second set. Then as they were clearing up Donny had slipped on the drum-sticks which Ruth had thrown irritably across to him. Whereupon all the boys had gone away and left her to have a party on her own, which had triggered her attempt to find female companionship in Manchester, with disastrous results.

Cheryl sat and stared out at the darkness, disturbed by the discovery that the quarrel had arisen because of her naivety in believing a liar like Donny. That she was partly responsible for Ruth's demise was a hard pill to swallow. Gripping the steering wheel she tapped out a tense rhythm with the first finger of each hand. She gave Ricky no other indication of her feelings.

"Need a lift anywhere?" she asked at last.

"I've got my bike. Thanks all the same."

And off he cycled, not knowing whether or not he had been wasting his time.

Ruth had a good many visitors. Band members came in pairs. Lucy had arranged it that way, knowing that Ruth could not chat and finding that one-sided conversations tended to peter out within minutes. It was frustrating for the patient, particularly when that patient was someone like Ruth, who was used to contributing her own views on the matter, to have to lie there silently. But if two people visited they could talk to one another and Ruth could listen.

Someone had provided the patient with a pad of paper and a biro so that she could make the odd laborious answer to direct questions. But she lacked the will to bother with light conversation. It was surprising how much you could leave unsaid when you confined yourself to essentials.

On her second visit Lucy brought Judith, who was a singing teacher. The pair of them spent the whole time talking about the music exam syllabus while Ruth drifted off to sleep.

Eileen arrived next, accompanied by her daughter Susie, who had very little to say, but who could at least be brought into the conversation in a monosyllabic capacity, as in "and then we saw the same thing much cheaper in Chorley Market, didn't we, Susie?"

"Yes Mum."

Rachel and Rebecca came by bus on Saturday afternoon. They had not really intended to tell her all about the dishy boys they knew and the goings on at the school bicycle sheds, but that was how it developed by the time they had lapsed into what was basically routine sisterly gossip, which is not to say that Ruth was unamused by it.

The three trombonists arrived together. Only two visitors were allowed at once, so they worked a rota which involved so much walking in and out and up and down corridors, together with explanations and corrections of one another that they hardly had time to talk to Ruth at all.

On Lucy's next visit she brought with her Sheena, the baritone horn player. The girl had brought Ruth some cigarettes, which Ruth regarded wistfully. Tobacco deprivation was one more discomfort to add to the general tally. But having now suffered the worst of the withdrawal symptoms, considerably lightened by all the painkillers and made trivial by the pain, she had decided to try and give up the habit if she could.

She returned the packet to Sheena with a scribbled note of thanks for the thought and Sheena lit one gratefully as soon as she could escape to the corridor, only to be caught and made to put it out by the staff nurse.

Soon after this Ruth was allowed to hobble around the ward with a stick for support. The plaster cast had been removed from her jaw, which was now held safely in shape by a wire contraption. When the hour for visitors arrived, she put her walking stick aside and sat up on the bedcovers, hoping someone would be free to come and see her. It always gave her a boost to see people from the outside world.

She entertained fantasies that Sarah would turn up. Were she and Nevil and the children living in cosy domestic bliss now? Or was he still cruel to her? Did Sarah know what had happened? Did she know where she was? Would she risk a visit if she did? Of course not.

However someone equally unexpected was among the stream of arriving vistors who came through the door; the only person who could, when she chose to, help her to draw a line under Sarah and get on with a life which, who knows, could be sunny again from time to time. It was Cheryl, of course, who appeared at her bedside, smiling as if she had never done otherwise and closely followed by Sally-the-bass.

"Hi!" Cheryl greeted her, handing over a large bunch of juicy black grapes.

Ruth looked at them ruefully. At the moment everything had to come through a straw. She gestured her two visitors to sit down. They at least could enjoy them. Her pleasure at Cheryl's visit was worth more than grapes.

"Is your jaw going to be okay?" asked Sally, eyes riveted on the metal frame around Ruth's chin.

Ruth shrugged carefully.

She was not cheered by the way Sally was looking at her. Was that going to be how she would be regarded by the public at large when once she could venture back to civilisation? Horror and pity? The metal structure had felt like a liberation after the plaster. She would like to have looked in the mirror to reassure herself it was not that bad. But all her mirrors had been taken away.

"They'd have been less rough if you hadn't put up such a fight," Cheryl advised her.

"Thanks," said Ruth wryly, through unmoving teeth.

She could talk a little now, in the manner of a ventriloquist. She was even able to join in the conversation. But it was largely unnecessary, since Cheryl kept up a near monologue on the subject of Raggle Taggle and all they were doing, what had happened in band lately and the preparations for the fete.

Sally in her boredom began leafing through *The British Bandsman* magazines which she had brought for Ruth to read.

On Ricky's next visit he was surprised at the change in her.

"You're looking much brighter! Are they going to let you out soon?"

"Not yet. This off first." She gestured towards her face.

"Wait until you see what I've brought you!" He reached inside his jacket and brought out a cheque. Ruth read it and was speechless.

"That single is making a bomb," he told her. "Who needs gold mines?"

"Good." She was going to need every penny when she left the cosy hospital for the harsh world outside.

She sat and held it in her hands. She continued to look at it while Ricky told her about the group's developments. Everything was moving fast, he said. He had given in his notice at his day job now and taken a flat with his friend Ray. The Stonemasons were having to fit in engagements at the nearby towns as well as the Granary and of course were able to ask a larger fee. A whole album of tracks was being put together and there were a couple more radio and TV dates in the pipeline.

"How's the saxophone?" Ruth wanted to know.

"He plays the same phrase all the time. But nobody seems to mind."

"That figures!"

"Get that cheque into your bank account," Ricky warned her. "Now that Collinson's our agent he's always trying to claim what we earn for expenses of some kind or another."

He did not add that he had had to battle to get her any money at all. They had tried to cut her out of the first heady share-out.

"Can you put it in for me?" she asked, knowing she could trust him.

She took a page from her note pad and wrote down the name of her bank and her account number. She added a message of her own. Then she folded it up with the cheque and pushed it into the top pocket of his jacket.

When later he stood at the bank counter he pulled out that piece of paper from his pocket. There, plain to read, along with her account number, were the words: *If ever you need me, shout. I'll be there.*

He had to smile at the thought of her debunking from the

hospital and coming to his rescue with her poor patched-up face.

The day before the frame was to be removed and she was to begin therapy to restore movement to her jaw, a svelte person walked like a fashion model into the day room where Ruth sat reading the problem page of a women's magazine. It was a new Annette. Previously she had just been beautiful, but now she was so well-groomed that Ruth caught herself wondering if she was real. A couple of old ladies with new hip-joints and a young girl with an arm in plaster who had been sitting around listlessly looked on with mouths slightly agape.

"House of Dior comes to Bolton Royal Infirmary!" exclaimed Ruth, rising to meet her and give her a hug.

"I could have died when they told me," her visitor began, "I can't turn my back for a minute, can I, without you getting yourself in a mess. How are you feeling?"

"Pleased to see you."

They sat creakily in the cane chairs of the sunlit room. Large windows overlooked gardens in the full flower of high summer. A spectacular Laburnum tree threw a yellow proscenium arch around the view.

"Are you going to be all right when they take that apology for modern sculpture off your face?"

"Modern sculpture needs a bigger apology than this."

"You know what I mean."

"There's a couple of teeth I'll never see again, but they seem to think it'll be all right eventually."

"Did the police ever catch anybody?"

Ruth shook her head.

"Don't feel too rotten about that," Annette advised her. "It's probably saved you from a nasty time in court."

"So," began Ruth, not wanting to pursue that depressing line of conversation, "tell me about Paris. Did you fall in love?"

"What makes you say that?"

"Don't tell me you did!"

Ruth had meant it as a joke, but Annette's face told her that it was no laughing matter.

"Let's go outside," suggested Annette. "Are you allowed outside?"

"If you give me your arm for support."

They wandered through the big window onto the patio, and leaned on a section of balustrade which overlooked the flower beds.

"Well?" asked Ruth at last.

Annette did not answer. She turned around, half-sat on the balustrade, folded her arms across her chest and studied her feet.

"He hasn't written and I may never see him again. It's hell. Have you got a cigarette?"

"No. I don't smoke now."

"Damn!" She turned around and faced the garden once more.

Ruth regarded her normally poised companion, whose eyes were now hidden by dark glasses.

"But what if he does write?" Ruth said. "What then? Would you go away again and not come back?"

11

One Thursday early in August, when summer was at its height and rain was an infrequent visitor, the wire scaffolding was at last removed from Ruth's face. She was checked over and allowed to leave the hospital. She was glad of her freedom, though she knew she was going to have to keep returning to the hospital's outpatients' department for some time to come to receive therapy to restore full movement to her jaw. Dental treatment would also be required. Her lower calf, which had had a mild greenstick fracture and extensive bruising, as though trampled upon, had been taken out of plaster some time ago. She was eager to return to the big world outside.

She was taken downstairs in the lift for the last time. Once on the ground floor, she called at the reception desk to order a taxi, but the bursar told her there was no need.

"There's a friend of yours waiting to give you a lift home," he told her, jabbing his pen towards an area of seating, which lay in an alcove behind a pillar.

It could not be Annette. She would be working in Manchester at this hour. 'Ricky!' thought Ruth. 'What would I do without him?'

But when she rounded the pillar by the waiting area it was not Ricky who rose from a chair to meet her but Cheryl.

"Hi!" was her greeting. "Have you got a case I can carry for you?"

"It's just there," said Ruth, pointing to the spot near the door where a medical orderly had put it for her.

They walked out into a hot late morning sunshine. Ruth paused on the pathway and turned her face upwards, taking in the air like a newly-released prisoner. The scent of wallflowers and lemon balm came to her from the herbaceous borders. The noise of traffic on the main road was a busy distant murmur. Everywhere there was sound, colour, movement. She was a part of the world again.

"Come on," urged Cheryl, not understanding why she was standing hesitating for so long. "I'm a careful driver."

They climbed into the Raggle Taggle van and Cheryl drove it with all due care out into the cut and thrust of the main road.

"I presume you want to go straight to Chorley?"

"Do you mind if we go through Rivington?" ventured Ruth on an impulse. "It's a bit further, but I have this longing for the open countryside."

"Sure. Where's your car now, anyway?"

"The police took it back for me. To the pokey little flat I call home. Are you all right for time?" she added, glancing at Cheryl's determined profile, her mouth pursed and eyes alert for all the ills the roads are heir to.

"I've got all day if you like. Daddy's given me a long weekend off."

The leafy lanes of Rivington were soothing after hospital and the busy built-up area through which they had just passed. She asked Cheryl to stop by a grove of oak and birch saplings where stately sweet chestnut trees cast a protective shade over the young stock. Cheryl climbed out of the driver's side and came around to help her jump out. Although Ruth felt she did not need it, she accepted Cheryl's hand as she put her mended leg on the ground. Side by side they strolled around the springy forest floor, touching the bark, snapping off a twig, listening to the birds and sniffing in the greenery. Cheryl took her arm and they walked around, pointing out a colourful bit of fungus here, an unusual plant there.

Ruth's appreciation of the ordinary was sharpened, like that of a child seeing something for the first time. The sight of a flapping crow, whose wings caressed the lower perimeter of their reach as though the air were sticky there, filled her with wonder.

But she began to feel tired, and Cheryl was hungry, so they climbed back into the van and drove to the village, where she was able to stock up on essential groceries to take home. Cream doughnuts oozing jam were on display, and liver paté sandwiches.

"I've got to have some of those."

"Some of which?"

"Everything."

"Think you can manage it?"

"Perhaps not. I'll just make do with a liver páté' sandwich for now."

Cheryl decided to have a cream doughnut and added a large bottle of coca-cola to share between them. They walked down to the church hall and sat and ate on the low wall where Ruth used to have her cigarettes. She took everything slowly, breaking off small pieces and eating them one by one.

Cheryl sat on the wall, not gracefully like Annette, but all elbows and knees. One hand drummed on the rugged stone while she used the other to shove the doughnut into her mouth with uninhibited relish.

"You've got some jam on your lip," Ruth told her, suddenly and illogically overtaken by happiness.

They strolled back arm in arm to where the faithful van waited like a good horse. But the sun was shining, so they took a rug from the vehicle and stretched out for a few minutes on the village green. Cheryl picked a stem of rye grass to chew.

"I gather the Stonemasons did the dirty on you," she began, carefully.

"I think they would have anyway, sooner or later," said Ruth philosophically, turning onto her side and combing through a clover patch in the unlikely hope of finding a lucky four-leaved one. "Donny and I never really got on. I was only there because I was useful."

"I don't think they deserved you."

"If there's any justice, they're about to find that out."

"So what will you do now?"

"I've got some money. My song is still making money."

"Yes, but what will you do? Write some more?"

"Writing them is one thing. Getting them in the charts is another. *Going Down* was in the right place at the right time, I guess."

"Will you write one for us?"

"I might."

"Barney and Roger are off to Cambridge very soon."

"So does that mean 'hurry up and write one' or does it mean I'll be wasting my time?"

"It means write one pronto. So we can get it on tape before they go."

"Hmm. Let's get back in the van. I ought to take that milk home before it goes sour."

This time they headed towards Chorley. Cheryl kept opening her mouth, then shutting it again. Finally she burst out.

"How would you feel about joining another group?"

Ruth's thoughts had been on her stomach. She was not ready to give a fully considered answer.

"I may never be able to play the trumpet any more," she cautioned.

"So? You'll be able to play guitar, won't you? You can play keyboard. You can set chords. You know the ropes. You're a name, whether Donny likes it or not."

"Names don't last long in this business," Ruth pointed out.

"They do if you build on them."

Ruth did not answer. She watched the grass verge flashing past. her stomach was not happy about the liver pate sandwich. She put a hand over her eyes. Her forehead was damp.

"I expect you think I'm rather a calculating person," hazarded Cheryl, misreading her silence.

"I know you're a calculating person," Ruth told her. "It's part of your charm."

"I'm not sure how to take that."

"Can you stop the van? I want to look at the reservoir. The fish are jumping. we should get a good view if you stop now"

"What? here?"

"Yes. here."

They were half way along the road between the reservoirs. Luckily there was not much traffic. Ruth concentrated on jumping fish and willed her stomach to behave. She dared not vomit. Even yawning was an activity she had to indulge in with care. Cheryl got out and came to join her.

"You're quite green," she said. "Lean on the wall here."

Ruth put her arms on the top of the wall and leaned her head on them and breathed in deeply the fresh watery air until things improved inside. Cheryl put a hand on her forehead.

"Is there anything I can get you?"

"No. I'll be all right now, I think, if you drive smoothly and with no jerking."

"I've got some brandy. You can have a shot of that," Cheryl said when they had climbed back in.

"Better not."

"Tell me if you want me to stop again."

"I will."

They drove past the Bay Horse at Heath Charnock and carefully down the cobbles of Babylon Lane. Cheryl wondered whether to remind her of the question, which she had not yet answered. Was she being too pushy?

They turned right at the crossroads and drove along the smooth tarmac of the main Chorley Road.

"Raggle Taggle are having a practice session tomorrow," Cheryl told her. "Why not come along and hear us? Get the feel of our style. If you want to give us the benefit of your opinion, we'd all of us be very pleased."

"Even though you're breaking up soon?"

"We'd enjoy it. Perhaps you might too."

"Want me to bring you a song then? Work on it with you?"

"Oh yes please, if you've got one."

Ruth had dozens, but not all of them would suit a group.

"You'll have to come and collect me. I don't feel ready to go out alone yet."

"Why don't we have lunch together? Make a day of it."

"I'd love that."

In the end they spent the rest of Thursday together as well. They checked over Ruth's car and, just to prove it was working all right, she drove it over the moor to a pub in Darwen where they sat and talked over a drink. Then they returned to Ruth's flat, where Cheryl's van was parked, picking up some fish and chips on the way. Cheryl ate them in Ruth's flat for her tea while Ruth settled for safety with one slice of toast (with the crusts removed) and marmalade, followed by a banana and a cup of tea.

Cheryl washed the dishes while Ruth rested on her lumpy sofa. She was supposedly watching the TV, but when Cheryl returned from the kitchen sink she found her stretched out fast asleep on two pillows and a cushion, which had been pressed into service to cover the uncomfortable lumps.

Cheryl had not the heart to wake her. She went out to her van, took a woollen spread from the back, returned to Ruth's lounge and covered the sleeping figure with it. Then she gave a silent wave from the doorway and tip-toed away.

The following day the two of them had lunch at the Jumping Trout, after which Cheryl drove Ruth to the Prescot-Withers' family home on the better side of Bolton, where Ruth was introduced to their music room. This had been taken over by Raggle Taggle for their practices. It used to be referred to as the junk room but had recently been commandeered by the younger generation and fitted up with many electrical sockets. A baby grand piano had been relegated to a corner to make way for Cheryl's drums as well as amplifiers and an electronic keyboard, stands, microphones, a good reel-to-reel tape recorder and all the paraphernalia a pop fanatic of the sixties could desire.

The walls had been sound-proofed to spare the parents' ears.

Ruth took one look at the baby grand and headed straight for it. The piano had been her first instrument. She had been the soloist in several piano concertos with an orchestra of fellow-students. In her final year she had been featured in Robert Schumann's passionate A minor concerto, playing from memory, to great acclaim. Since she had left home there had been no piano in her life and she was hungry for the keys. She climbed over some equipment and gently lifted the lid. It was a Bluthner. Oh joy!

The piano stool was nowhere to be seen, so she stood before the keyboard and arpegiated from bottom to top, then back again. The tuning was tolerable.

She turned round. Cheryl was watching her in some surprise.

"That's not what we came for," she said.

"Can't you humour an invalid?"

"All right, go ahead, but let's fit in some of our music as well."

So Ruth decided she would warm up with one of Schubert's last piano sonatas, only to discover that she was too rusty to play to anywhere near to the standard she had once achieved. Sadly but gently, she closed the lid and gave herself over to Cheryl's agenda.

Barney and Roger turned up late in the afternoon. The first thing they did was rescue the piano stool from under many objects. They placed it to one side of the central area for Ruth to sit on while she listened to the boys play one of their well-practised numbers. They had obviously gone to some pains to be musically correct and they had an intelligent approach to matters like tempo contrast. But she found them rather pale and sedate after the gritty Stonemasons.

"You've got to decide whether to please yourselves or your audience," she told them when they'd finished. "You've got talent but not enough pizzaz."

"Pizzaz? What do you mean, pizzaz?"

"It's one of those factors that grabs an audience and makes them howl for more. You recognise it instantly when it's there."

She gave them the song she had brought. It was a laid-back number for solo voice alternating with vocal backing from the rest of the band. It was called The Cat that Walks Alone. They picked up the melody quickly enough, since it was predictable and quite repetitive, and they followed the chords she had written out ready for them. She asked Cheryl to keep the steady walking-beat light during the solo vocals, but not be afraid to put in some fancy work between the singing. Then she picked up her guitar and joined them for a run-through.

"I'll cut out the rhythm guitar, I think," she said when they had finished.

"But you're playing rhythm guitar."

"I know. I'm out of practice. I may come in on the second chorus. Be more effective then. I can still sing. Put the tape on and try it. You'll see what I mean. Start with the introduction – just bass and drums at first. Or better still, just a crescendo roll on the side drum; then hit three crotchets to set up the tempo.

There's a double quaver upbeat which I'll come in on, then everybody come in on the downbeat of the next bar. Try it."

It was a mess, since they were all still trying to work out what she had been talking about.

"Listen," she explained. "My first line is: *If you want to know where to find me*. So. Cheryl hits three crotchets… Da! Da! Da!… '*if you* want'. You come in on want. Let's try again."

They did and their timing was perfect.

"What about the right hand?" asked Barney's friend Roger when they had finished. He was playing the bass line on his keyboard with his left hand, because their bass player, Jason, had gone for a job interview in Birmingham. Roger's right hand was free.

She stood behind him and held her right hand over the upper keys.

"Put in that bass introduction I've given you. Not too loud, it's only a cat!"

He did so and she improvised a few chords over it. "How about this?" she played them again and made him copy them a couple of times. "Work on your own version, if you like. Pity you can't get up into the piccolo range. That'd be more feline. Not a very big keyboard, is it."

"So you want to buy me a better one?"

"Sorry, no. But nice try. Anyway let's hear it with the lyric."

Later Ruth and Cheryl sat in the sun and enjoyed a milk shake on the ample Prescott-Withers lawn while the young men went off for a swim.

"What's Annette Mackenzie doing these days?" asked Cheryl. "She hasn't been to band yet."

"I think she wanted some time to get her playing lip working again. She'll be there on Wednesday, so she told me."

"Lucy will be pleased."

"I know. The fete's a fortnight tomorrow, I gather."

"You going to be there?"

"The fete? Yes. I shall come."

It was going to be painful. She had picked up her cornet that morning and blown it gingerly in her thin-walled flat. But her poor old face had taken too much punishment. Her tone was gone, her lips had lost resilience. She seemed to have lost all the embouchure which she used to have. She would have to watch from the wings and that would hurt.

"Come and see me after the practice on Wednesday," she suggested. "When you've dropped off all your passengers. Tell me how it went and I'll give you a coffee."

"Okay I will."

They watched a couple of swallows wheeling low over the grass. A sign of rain. "How would Annette feel about playing in our group?"

"Honestly, Cheryl, you're priceless!"

"I don't see why. "

"She'd certainly provide the 'pizzaz' standing up front, if that's what you had in mind."

"Ah! Now I know what you mean by 'pizzaz'."

"But she's got three children and a very time-consuming job, which she enjoys."

"You could always ask her."

"Asking her is something you'll have to do for yourself. But I'll sound her out if it will help."

"It would help. Really. I'd be grateful."

The Major appeared with an armful of baskets and canvas carrier bags. He was wearing a Panama sun hat.

"Look lively, you two. We're going to pick up windfalls in the orchard before it rains and rots them. Where's Barney?"

"Gone for a swim, wouldn't you know it."

They hauled themselves out of comfy wooden garden chairs into which the sun had seemed to glue them. They followed the Major, taking a basket each, and proceeded to comb the grass for eatable apples. Ruth hated slugs. Most of the windfalls were home to at least one. But she did not complain and her reward was to be asked to stay to tea.

It was a lively meal, with Barney and Roger there, making six. Ruth was introduced to Mrs Prescott-Withers, a quiet, vague woman, who seemed content to be ordered about by her husband and children. She had the same fine blue eyes as Cheryl, but none of her daughter's forthright personality, or none that could be detected on so brief an acquaintance.

By mid-evening Ruth was feeling exhausted again. It was a happy exhaustion but one that forced her eventually to call it a day.

"Come on, then," said Cheryl. "I'll take you back."

"You can come in for a drink."

"Just don't fall asleep on me this time."

"That reminds me. I must return the rug you were so kind as to leave me."

"You looked like you would be there for the night."

"I was, actually. But not this time, I think."

The next day Annette invited herself round to see Ruth's new flat. She was not impressed. She sat gingerly in one of the shabby armchairs and gazed around at the mismatched furnishings.

"How can you bear it?"

Ruth forced open the small window to let out the smell of damp. Instead it let in all the petrol fumes.

"Ricky brought me another cheque yesterday," she said. "I think I might put a down payment on a boarding house somewhere. Run it with a staff, perhaps. It would give me some security."

"Have to be on the coast," advised Annette, "if you want people to spend their holidays in it. Shall I ask Harold if he's seen anything worth going for?"

"If you're still speaking to him."

"He doesn't know."

"If you want my opinion, I think you'd be mad to leave Harold. He's given you so much. You could get left high and dry with your life in wreckage around you. Believe me, I know all about wreckage. Don't do it."

"I know all that. I know all that." She looked unseeing at the wall.

"You've had a letter, haven't you?"

"Yes."

"And he wants you to leave Harold and go to him."

"That's right."

"And the children?"

"Ah yes, the children. Something would have to be sorted out."

"We can't go on living by our emotions, you know," Ruth advised her. "We're not schoolgirls any more. You have responsibilities. You said it yourself. When you have children, you've got to put yourself second. Don't go chasing rainbows. I wouldn't want you to suffer like Sarah suffered."

But was she trying to convince Annette? Or was she trying to convince herself? For Annette there was such a thing as divorce and re-marriage. She could even share custody of the children. No court would refuse her access to them, simply for living with another man.

"Don't worry," sighed Annette. He's too young anyway. It could ruin both our lives.

"How young is too young?"

He's as much younger than me as Harold is older. Work that out."

Ruth worked it out. "Mmmm," she said.

I'd forgotten how much it can hurt," Annette told her, "to say 'No' when you long to say 'Yes'.

Faint lines could be discerned on her forehead and under her eyes, the first small cracks in a crumbling facade. Ruth felt

117

sad for her and for all those who try to hold onto a happiness too insubstantial for mere humans to handle; that filters away like sunshine through a sieve, leaving a person bereft. She filled her own glass and watched the golden sun go down over Chorley's ugly black rooftops, beautifying the chimneys and illuminating the television aerials briefly before the onward march of darkness.

12

It was about half past ten when Cheryl drove up to Ruth's flat after transporting several players home from the brass band practice on Wednesday. A small Fiat was taking up the space next to the Hillman Minx, so Cheryl left her van further down the street, hoping it would come to no harm. It was the kind of area where aerials were snapped off and spare wheels could disappear if they were visible.

When she was admitted by Ruth, she saw that Annette was there before her.

"Hi!" she greeted her. She was pleased. This was her opportunity to put across her plans for the new group, and to offer Annette a place amid its ranks. "Is that your Fiat?"

"'I'm afraid so," responded Annette without warmth. Her thoughts were not musical ones at this time. There were things she still wanted to discuss with Ruth, but not if Cheryl was there. She stood up.

"Please don't move your car for me," protested Cheryl, "I've found a place to park quite close by."

"I must go, anyway," Annette assured her. "It's late. Harold will be imagining all sorts of things."

"Now what sort of things could he possibly imagine?" Ruth

could be heard to say, with a note of reproach in her voice, as she saw her to the outer door.

Annette's reply was short but inaudible to Cheryl.

Ruth returned and gestured to Cheryl to sit on the sofa, which was as lumpy as a child's Christmas stocking and far less inviting. But she sat on it as directed, rising again instantly to thump about its seating area in the hope of finding a more comfortable spot to put herself.

"I hope I wasn't interrupting anything," she said.

"Like what, for instance?"

Cheryl turned bright red.

"Like a conversation, of course," she hastened to say.

"I asked you round for coffee, remember," Ruth pointed out, with a little smile. "That means I was expecting you."

It was not easy to disconcert Cheryl, but it could be done.

"I was hoping Annette would stay for a chat."

"So that you could tell her about this fabulous new group you're planning?"

"Now you're laughing at me."

"No. Well not really. Black or white?"

"White. With brown sugar, if you have it."

"I have it."

Ruth disappeared into the kitchen area. Cups clattered. The kettle sang. Cheryl looked around the room. How could Ruth live in a place like this? There was damp around the skirting boards and hardly any natural light. The wallpaper may have looked nice before the first world war, but had suffered numberless mishaps since. The carpet was so dark and worn it was impossible to tell what the original pattern was; if indeed it had had one. It looked chewed at the edges. Did the building have rats? They would not have seemed out of place here.

"Couldn't you find a better hole to go to than this one?" she called out.

120

Ruth came in with two steaming mugs of instant coffee. It was easier than fiddling around with a tray and tiny cups and strainers and percolators and all the paraphernalia which making 'authentic' coffee entailed.

"At the time I moved in here I simply didn't care."

"How was that then?"

"You don't want to know, Cheryl."

It was plain from Cheryl's questioning manner that she did want to know, but Ruth had no intention of spoiling her evening by talking about Sarah. She placed the mugs of coffee on a small table next to the sofa.

"Want anything to eat?" she asked.

Cheryl shook her head

"I suppose you haven't mentioned to Annette… what I asked you to mention?" she ventured, moving a cushion and trying to find a more comfortable area of sofa.

"If I put it to her now she'd give a straight no. If you're wise, you'll wait, my little juggernaut. Learn a bit of patience from one who is older and I hope wiser."

Ruth sat next to her and handed her a mug. She wished that she could do something about the cardboard boxes with which the sofa appeared to have been stuffed.

"What did Barney have to say about my song?" she asked. "Be frank."

"He liked it. They both did. It's a pity they're not going to be here long enough to work on it properly. But it's all good experience and maybe we can keep it for the new group."

"So tell me. Who are you going to enlist? What are you planning to call it? Are you intending to keep the name Raggle Taggle?"

Three questions were more than enough to keep Cheryl talking while Ruth sipped her coffee and fixed her eyes upon her and wondered whether she dare run her hand up through the short hair on the back of her neck as she was tempted to do.

Cheryl looked up from her mug and intercepted Ruth's gaze. She stopped in mid-sentence.

Both mugs were placed on the table. Ruth put out a finger and ran it round Cheryl's ear. Cheryl took her wrist and pulled her closer until their lips were a couple of millimeters apart. Ruth closed the gap, gently meeting soft lips with a tentative mouth, and gently easing Cheryl backwards. Cheryl reached up and put both arms round Ruth's neck and, finding herself on a particularly uncomfortable part of the couch, she struggled to rise. Ruth sat up, nursing her jaw and cursing quietly, while Cheryl regained her feet and stood up to stretch, holding her back with the agonised expression of a gardener who has just cleared a path of weeds.

"Isn't there a decent bed in this ghastly dump?" she complained.

"Come and see." Ruth invited her, glad of an excuse to seek greater comfort than that which her sofa would ever afford.

She took Cheryl's hand and led her towards the bedroom.

It was at that point that the phone chose to ring.

The phone? It was after eleven by now. Few people knew Ruth's new number. The pair of them stood there hand in hand, as still as victims of Medusa, waiting for it to stop. But it went on.

"Are you going to answer it or not?" prompted Cheryl in the end.

"It must be someone for the previous occupant," Ruth said at last, dropping Cheryl's hand. "I'll get rid of them. Go on in. I'll be with you in a sec."

It was Ricky.

"Where were you? What kept you? I thought you were dead."

"It's a bit late, that's all."

"I know. Listen. I have to talk." His voice sounded choked. "Can you talk?"

"I... what do you mean, talk?" she hedged, desperately wanting to get rid of him, but not to give him the cold shoulder. He would not have phoned unless it was important. They never phoned each other just for a chat. Even teetering as she was on the slippery slope above the dark and dangerous waters of desire, she knew that she had to listen to him, as he would always have listened to her.

"I need somewhere to stay tonight," his voice continued into her silence. "I need someone to help me. Have you got room?"

Her heart sank. She saw the waters of desire receding like an ebbing tide over a flat stretch of sand. She wanted to screech, 'Not now. Any time but now!' But she could not brush away the consciousness of all he had done for her. Had he not brought her those all-important cheques on which she was surviving? Had she not scribbled '*If ever you need me shout. I'll be there.*'?

Well now he was shouting.

"What's happened?" she asked.

There was no reply for two or three seconds, only some gulping noises and she realised with a pang that he was crying.

"I can't tell you now. Can I come and see you?"

"Now?"

"Yes."

There was only one answer and Ruth had to bite the bullet and give it.

"Of course."

She made her way back to the bedroom, reflecting with regret that people never invited themselves around in the lonely evenings when a person was longing for company.

Cheryl, having taken off her shoes and bounced about a little on the bed to check that there were no uncomfortable lumps, was sitting up and in the act of pulling her top over her head. She stopped with one arm in and one out, peering through the neck-hole like a hesitant mouse.

"What's the matter?" she wanted to know, as Ruth came through the doorway much too slowly and thoughtfully for the business in hand.

"That was Ricky."

"Is something wrong?"

"Seems to be. He's in a state."

Cheryl voiced nothing, but her whole attitude was questioning. She swung her legs over the side of the bed. Ruth sat beside her and helped her to put her arm back through the empty sleeve and pulled straight the rumpled back for her.

"He's on his way here." She kissed her carefully on the cheek. "We haven't got time."

"How long before he gets here, then?" cried Cheryl, pulling away and pushing her feet back into her shoes.

"I don't know. I'm sorry, sweetheart. I didn't want him to come. But he's in trouble."

Cheryl's face closed up as if it had shutters. She rose and grabbed her jacket.

"What are you doing?" cried Ruth. "Are you leaving?"

"First it's Annette, then it's me, then it's Ricky. How many others have you got dangling around?"

"That wasn't very nice."

"What do you expect me to think? Look at the time! Is he going to stay the night?"

"He might. If he does it will not be in bed with me. And there's nothing like that between Annette and me either. You are the only one I want. And I've been living a totally chaste life for some time now, in case you're interested."

"I'm not interested," she swept towards the door. Ruth caught her arm.

"You don't have to go. I don't want you to go. Ricky won't mind if you stay. But I can't turn him away. He's always been there for me. I can't let him down."

Cheryl shook the hand off her arm. Ruth barred her way.

"Would you mind stepping aside, please?" snapped Cheryl in her father's voice.

"I can't let him down," repeated Ruth. "He's always been there for me. I wish I could make you understand."

"I understand perfectly," Cheryl told her. "Now can I get by, please?"

Ruth stepped aside and let her go. The outer door slammed. She went to the window and saw her walk down the street without a backward glance. Annette was right. She was obnoxious. And it hurt intensely.

She had a few minutes to clear away the cups and calm down a little before an urgent rapping on the door announced the next visitor. She opened it at once and Ricky almost fell in. There was blood all over his head and most of his clothes. A handkerchief had absorbed so much that it just looked like a cake of blood as he held it in his left hand pressed against his right forearm.

Ruth did not waste time asking questions. She led him straight to the bathroom where she ran the cold tap.

"Wash that face, Ricky, while I get the scissors."

She picked up a wad of cotton wool from her dressing table, her oldest towel from the linen cupboard and the antiseptic from the medicine cabinet. She gave him a chair, sat him down and handed him the towel to hold over his face with his left hand. She then cut the sleeve away from his right arm. There was a jagged slash mark from wrist almost to elbow.

"What a mess!"

He did not reply. He looked very pale. She ran a glass of water.

"Keep drinking that."

He winced a good deal while she dabbed at his arm. The knife had gone deep, but it seemed to have missed arteries and tendons. Once the blood had been stanched and wiped away, the wound was revealed as less serious than she had feared.

"You'll have to get it stitched," she told him. "What happened?"

"Can you just bandage it up for now?"

"There's some antiseptic on its way. Brace yourself."

He screamed and swore.

"Can I drive you to the emergency unit?"

"I'll see the doctor tomorrow."

"Where will you stay tonight? Can you go home?"

"My mam would have a heart attack. Or my dad would get the police. Both, I expect. Aaaagh! That hurt!"

Ruth regarded him. He was pale and trembling and his clothes were unfit for public view.

"Did Ray do this?"

Ricky nodded.

"You ought to inform the police, before he does it again and kills somebody."

"He won't. He isn't like that. It was my fault. I threw his supply into the loo pan and flushed it away. He went for me."

"Don't go back to him, Ricky."

"I couldn't. He threw me out."

"Where's all your clothes? Your guitar? All that."

"At the flat."

"I'll drive you there. We'll take your car. Save messing up mine as well. We'll pick up your stuff and come back here."

"What if…?"

"Never say 'what if.' We'll deal with what we find as and when we find it."

Fortunately when they drove up gingerly, there was no sign of anybody. Ricky unlocked the door and crept in, with Ruth following. Ray, presumably, was out looking for another 'supply'. They picked up as many of Ricky's clothes as they could fit into two suitcases, then returned for his guitars, his toothbrush, his portable radio, one or two records and an expensive alarm clock which had been a twenty-first birthday present. Anything else could wait.

"Good job it was my right arm," gritted Ricky through clenched teeth. The pain was really beginning to bite. "I should still be able to play the guitar."

"I think you'd better wait until you've had it seen to. What will you tell the doctor if he asks what happened?"

"I'll say I had an argument with a pane of glass."

Ricky spent a restless night on the armchair, which was slightly more comfortable than the sofa. Ruth gave him a cushion, a blanket and the spare pillow and left him to try to sleep. He would go back to his parents tomorrow when he looked fit to face them and move back in. They did not know about his lifestyle, any more than her parents knew about hers.

She climbed into her own bed and spent a couple of hours nursing the hurt of the things which Cheryl had said to her. But at least Ricky's troubles had taken her mind off her own. She would feel better tomorrow. Or the day after, perhaps.

In the morning she fed Ricky coffee and cooked him a breakfast and let him make free with her bathroom. She then put his right arm in a sling and he wore his clean jacket over it, the sleeve hanging loose. He was pale and red-eyed, a large piece of sticking plaster covered some of his forehead. Even his own mother could not call him handsome. His face was thin and his ears stuck out. His eyelashes and eyebrows were too pale, his chin too receding. But those who saw the kindness in his eyes forgot the rest.

He bit into a piece of toast and surveyed the room.

"Do you like this place?" he asked, eyeing an area of peeling wallpaper which failed to cover a damp patch on the wall.

"I don't intend to stay here long. I'm thinking of getting my own place."

"Buying, instead of renting?"

"With the money from *Going Down*. A going down-payment, you might call it"

She poured him some more coffee.

"If you and I pooled our resources," he told her, "we could

get quite a decent property and divide it into two. Make it self-contained, you understand," he added hastily. "Not living together. I'm not suggesting that."

"I would be flattered if you were, Ricky. Though of course I'd say no. But two flats is a good idea."

She sat down opposite him and poured some coffee for herself.

"We'd be close at hand for one another whenever needed," she observed wryly.

He managed a smile.

"We'd have to agree on the district and the price and everything. We'd need parking for at least two cars."

"Four cars, preferably… for our many visitors… and separate entrances if possible and no shared kitchen or bathroom," added Ruth. She wanted to be able to let it out if she were ever to return to the parental home some time in the future. She also wanted to have her own house as a bolt-hole, to retain her independence.

"Get it all set out legally," continued Ricky.

"Naturally." The idea grew better and better. "Shall I look around for a few places, while you're getting that arm seen to and sorting things out at home? Then we can discuss it again in a couple of days' time."

"Yes. Do that," he said. "Get lists of properties which are on the market from all the estate agents. Phone me. We'll fix a time and look at them together."

He left, if not a happier man, then at least one with a more positive outlook on life.

For the next two days Ruth was able to take her mind off Cheryl by making a full time job of house-hunting. There is a limit to the number of properties you can see in one day and she was determined to be thorough. She armed herself with all the relevant details that the estate agents could furnish her with and worked through the information systematically at her flat, deciding which houses to look at and which were altogether unsuitable.

At the end of each day she phoned Ricky to fill him in on what she had seen and what she had thought of what she had seen. Then together they decided which were worth looking at again at the weekend. She went home and spent some time on the telephone arranging with the agents a convenient time to look over each one. It was a healing therapy for both of them. It gave them time to put their distressing experiences behind them.

By Friday Ruth's preoccupation with available properties had given her enough distance from recent events for her to be able to view them with some perspective. She began to see what had passed between herself and Cheryl in a different light. Now that the seductive miasma of desire had settled down, clarity of vision returned, which revealed starkly that her response to Ricky's distress call, while being the only thing to do, had been extremely unkind to Cheryl.

Moreover, she had neither known nor cared about the girl's history. How experienced was Cheryl in these matters? Did she know what was coming? What effect would it have on her? Would it turn her into someone like herself? Being a social misfit was not a happy way to live. It was so easy to regard Cheryl's self-confidence as being indestructible. But there was once a girl called Ruth Anderton who had been just as sure of herself. Before Sarah took over her life she had been a girl who had earned plaudits wherever she went and whose future had shone golden with the promise of success.

'Now look at me,' she thought, and feelings of shame began to assail her. Did she want to turn Cheryl into a suicidal outcast like herself? Did she want to ruin her life, as her own had been ruined? Cheryl without her self-belief would be like a sea-bird without wings. Tragic. She probably had little idea what an affair with another woman involved in social terms. She would not have realised how much it would reduce her standing in many circles of society. It could jeopardise her hope of success. Better for her that she should stay ignorant.

Some time soon, she suspected, Cheryl might try to get back on friendly terms, if only for the sake of her new group. It would surely not be long before her ambition triumphed over her pride. When that happened Ruth must try to keep their relationship under control. In other words - hands off! She would attempt no peace-making overtures of her own. But if Cheryl was prepared to apologise for what she had said and still wanted her friendship, then she would give her friendship. But only friendship.

13

It was the day of the church fete and the morning was fair, but with a feel that the weather had not made up its mind about the afternoon. Ricky and Ruth decided to take advantage of the favourable conditions, while they lasted, to view a batch of properties. Ricky wolfed down some breakfast and drove straight to the grim block which housed Ruth's flat. He was driving an incredibly long, defiantly pink convertible, all shiny and new. He pulled to a halt along the gutter with as much enthusiasm as a woman in a wedding dress venturing into a muddy field.

They had made little progress with their house-hunting so far. Any place that was large enough was too expensive. If it was not too expensive it was sited near a gas works or a railway station. If it was well-situated it was too far away from where they wanted to be. They were both beginning to wonder whether it was a bad idea to buy a place together. But neither wanted to be the first to say so.

"There are four properties," Ruth told him, climbing into the splendid machine and slamming the door. "I love your new car."

"Thank you. So do I. Bought it outright with my last cheque."

"What did you do with your old one?"

"I traded it in, bloodstains and all."

"That must have reduced its value."

"Practically gave it away. I don't care. I can afford it. We charge huge sums for our gigs now. Not just the ones at Granary, but all the other places. Collinson says he's getting enquiries from all over the country and if we don't tour soon we'll miss out on the opportunity."

"Turn left here," said Ruth. She did not want to hear about the success from which she had been excluded.

They managed to give three places the going-over, without seeing anything that appealed to them. The first place was a bit too close to a quarry for Ricky's liking, the second was way too small and the third was sandwiched between a primary school and a housing estate. They turned back to the car, longing for a coffee or, better still, something stronger.

"There's one more place I've arranged to visit," Ruth told him. "It's on the edge of Rivington."

"Not far from Annette, I bet."

"Does that matter?"

"As long as it suits me as well."

Ruth unfolded the paper with the agent's description of it.

"It's a Georgian four-bedroomed house, set in half an acre of land on the borders of Rivington and Anderton. A stream runs along its lower boundary. It has a well-kept, mature garden, four bedrooms and a second toilet downstairs." Ruth read out. "Hey, it's even got an ornamental pond with a fountain," she added.

"Highjinks for our summer parties!" enthused Ricky.

"For *your* summer parties, you mean."

It seemed just what they wanted. But when they arrived at the location Ricky would not even get out of the car.

"It's a great pity," he explained, "but I happen to know that they're going to put the motorway through here. I reckon that house is going to be stuck on the edge of it, if not in the middle, even."

They moved off, with the feeling of failure hovering like a bird of night over their heads. Ricky took a short cut through a lane which would take them straight onto the main Chorley Road. On the right they passed a five-barred gate over a track well churned-up by cattle hooves. A 'For Sale' notice was stuck beside it at a rakish angle. Ricky stood on the brakes and reversed back. The gate sported a name-plate on which the words *Pigham's Farm* could just be made out.

"Where's the farm-house?"

Ricky pulled into the side to leave enough room for other vehicles to pass, switched off the engine and climbed out. Ruth had to clamber over the gear lever and the driver's seat in the most ungainly manner before emerging onto terra firma. She joined Ricky where he was leaning with his elbows on the gate. At the other side of the field, amid a cluster of trees, stood a long building of sturdy millstone grit. Even at this distance they could see that the gutters sagged, the path was overgrown and several windows were broken. The roof ridge dipped badly, a sign that the timbers underneath it were rotten. Dark squares told them that many of the tiles were missing.

"It's got plenty of land," said Ruth, trying to look on the bright side. "Where is this place we're in?"

"Anderton. We've just passed the boundary."

"Anderton!" Ruth's heart beat faster. 'My name's Anderton,' she thought. Aloud she said, "Let's take a closer look."

Ricky succeeded in pushing open the gate and they picked their way over the mud and across the field. The closer they drew, the more faults they could see. But it was a sturdy well-built edifice which had the comfortable look of a house that felt at home in its surroundings. Across its yard stood a disused hay barn constructed of the same stone.

Ruth fell in love with it there and then.

"It's just the right size," she said, "and in just the right place. I wonder what they're asking for it."

"Find out, then we'll offer them half," said Ricky, who liked the situation and the building, but not the state it was in.

"Shall we go ahead and fix a time to view?"

"If you like. But bear in mind we couldn't move straight in. I could see it needed a complete renovation even before we crossed the field to look at it."

Ruth noted down the telephone number of the estate agent which was given on the *For Sale* sign and they climbed back into Ricky's car. Suddenly the day was brighter. They drove downhill onto the Chorley road, singing in harmony to the tune of Going Down, a version that might have pleased Donny, had that been its purpose:-

'Never felt so good, now we're out of the gloomy wood,' sang Ruth.

'And we're making good ground, on the merry-go-round,' added Ricky.

"That doesn't make sense," she told him.

"Does it matter?"

"Well if it doesn't matter to you, it doesn't matter to me."

"Ok. It's your line next."

'Where it's in for a penny or in for a pound.'

"That's rubbish," he said.

So they sang the 'going down' chorus as they went down the hill, then they oo-bi doo-bied their way through the second verse. By the time they reached Ruth's flat the sun was shining, making Chorley look uncharacteristically cheerful.

"Want to come in for a coffee?" Ruth invited him.

"No thanks. Got some shopping to do."

She climbed out. He tooted the horn and drove away.

As Ruth turned the key in the lock of the outer door, she could hear her phone ringing. Her heart pounding, she fumbled with her key, rushed in and managed to reach it before it stopped. It was Lucy.

"Are you coming this afternoon?"

"Yes. I'm planning to."

"I wonder if I can ask you a favour."

"As long as you don't expect me to play."

"No. Nothing like that. It's just that Sally's husband is in hospital and she needs someone to keep an eye on her two little boys while she plays. Only while she plays. It won't be for the whole afternoon. The band isn't the only entertainment there's going to be."

"I don't mind doing that. Will they mind being taken around by a strange lady?"

"Come early and be introduced."

So she got there half an hour before the band was due to play, in time for Sally to hand over her children in person. Mark was nearly five and Jamie was two. The boys obediently said hello to 'Aunty Ruth' and stood nicely until the moment came for Sally to join the rest of the band, when Jamie let out a yell and ran after his mother. Mark caught him and led him back, his little mouth turned down at the corners.

Ruth let them each choose a toffee from the bag of wrapped sweets she had brought with her. Then she led them to a position where they could see Sally and wave to her, as the band assembled.

When the two boys had accepted that their mother was not going to be taken away and put in the hospital, like daddy, Ruth led them off to where the public thronged the hoopla stalls and the coconut shies. There was a lucky dip and a mobile ice-cream van and even a small roundabout for the very young. By the time they had ridden on that they had lost any shyness.

"What happened to your face?" asked Mark with childish candour.

"It got broken. It had to be stuck together again."

"Did it hurt?"

"Yes, lots. At first. It's all right now."

The band had continued to fill the air with the pleasant

summer sound of outdoors brass. Ruth led them closer in that direction. It was the first time the boys had actually seen their mother play with the others.

All the chairs which were not needed for the players had been set out in rows for those members of the public who just wanted to sit and listen. Barney and Roger lounged on the grass wearing identical T-shirts that bore the legend Roll up here for the brassy airs!

The joke would have been more apparent had they succeeded in selling their idea to the ladies of the band.

The Major and Mrs Prescott-Withers sat a couple of rows back dressed fit to attend a Buckingham Palace garden party. In a break between numbers several similar people came to sit near them, exchanging greetings and pleasantries in penetrating voices, rising and pecking one another's cheeks and then sitting down again.

The band struck up next with the Medley of Scottish Airs. Ruth could not believe it. How could they play it without her? She was overtaken by a pang of grief for her lost skill. But they missed out the cornet cadenza. That was some consolation. She picked up Jamie and gave him a piggy back, the better to see his mother, while she herself listened out for Annette's Comin' thru' the Rye. Annette could see her out there watching among the crowd and went and cracked the top note. Hell!

Ruth would like to have watched for longer, but Mark was impatient to be sampling some of the treats on offer, so she allowed him to lead her away. The strains of the melodies which should have been hers kept pace with her mockingly all round the side shows. It did hurt. But she had to admit that the players were making a good sound. She must be sure to say as much to Lucy afterwards.

"What'll you have?" came a voice at her elbow. It was Harold Mackenzie. He stood a few yards from the drinks tent nursing a Pimms. He was watching the band from a judicious distance.

"A lemonade would be most welcome."

She swung Jamie to the ground and he laughed and hung onto her arm, wanting to be swung again.

"And something for the boys?"

"Want a fizzy drink, Mark?"

"Oooh yeah!"

He bought each of them the soft drink of their choice.

"You're a pal, Harold Mackenzie," said Ruth, drinking like the children, through a straw stuck in the bottle.

"Bit of an unfamiliar role for you, isn't it?" his grey eyes with their dark lashes surveyed her quizzically. "Children's nanny?"

"Oh well," she hedged, not sure how she was supposed to take that. "Anything to help out."

Two of his own children ran up and demanded a quenching of their thirst and he was occupied again. Ruth hung around for a while and tried to return his banter out of courtesy, though she was never quite at ease with him, never sure whether or not he was getting at her. But now that they were on the same side, whether he knew it or not, she had to admit that he gave a girl a feeling of security.

The clusters of young men standing around quite innocently drinking struck a nasty chord in the basso profundo regions of her consciousness. There was a sudden burst of male laughter and she jumped like a startled cat. Then she felt Harold's hand press her shoulder and instead of making her start away it gave her a feeling that she was safe as long as he was there. Lucky Annette! Why did she not know it?

After the band had run out of repertoire they put away their instruments, folded their music stands and made way for a troupe of little girls in pretty costumes who were to entertain with some formation dancing. While the change-over was taking place, the vicar took over the public address system and asked for a round of applause for Lucy Brindle's Ladies

137

Band. There was a spattering of polite clapping from those who had heard him. As with most ad hoc amplification systems the diction became smudged as soon as the volume rose and the sound would grow and fade because the person at the microphone was too inexperienced to keep his head still. Ruth piggy-backed Jamie again and took Mark's hand to guide them closer to the platform so that she could hear the vicar's voice without the amplification.

He was telling the throng how pleased he was to have been able to offer Lucy's band the Rivington Church Hall in their hour of need; how the whole congregation was now sharing the benefits of having them there; how they had provided the fete with the perfect music to accompany a joyful outdoor occasion on a summer's day. He hoped this would be the first of many such. He told them how much he had come to enjoy listening to them on their Wednesday evening practice nights.

"I always know when it's Wednesday," he concluded, "because of the splendid sounds coming from the Church Hall; sounds which can be heard quite clearly from the vicarage. I sometimes walk out onto my lawn, if the evening is fine, and I stand for a while and listen to those sounds and I thank God in all his goodness for the gift of music. To have it brought to one at one's doorstep, so to speak, is a great blessing."

His audience clapped and murmured its appreciation of Lucy Brindle's Band.

He went on to give the troupe of dancers a glowing introduction, then turned from the public address system to let the entertainment proceed. Ruth saw that Sally was bass-free and helping to dismantle the percussion, so she returned Mark and Jamie to their mum.

"Any news?" she asked her solicitously.

Sally shook her head, without speaking. Cheryl put a finger to her lips as a sign to Ruth not to talk about it in front of the children. It was the first communication they had had since the night of Ricky's visit. Did that mean Ruth was back in favour? Did she want to be?

Feeling a twinge of anger that Cheryl could look so insouciant after the pain she had caused, Ruth turned away to where Lucy, pink in the face, was collecting music and accepting the eulogies of many people. Even the father of Rachel and Rebecca, who was a brass band fanatic, had given the conductor a nod and a smile in order to be encouraging without committing himself to praise. He had found the sound a bit thin and lacking in crispness, which was only to be expected, with so many absentees, but quite good 'for lasses'.

"I'm sorry to say, Lucy," Ruth told her when she could get her attention, "that you seem to be managing extremely well without me."

"Thank you, Ruth, if that was the compliment I think it was. I'm glad to see you out and about again. We've missed you."

She noted that Ruth was looking pale and thin. Her hair had grown just enough to restore a layer of mop to her head. It had become more curly now that it was growing again. But it did little to hide the scar on her face that might never go. It must have taken courage to get back to mingling with the common herd after the kind of experience she had suffered.

They exchanged more polite enquiries as to the state of various people's well-being, before Lucy turned away to attend to the business of making sure that all the sheet music was collected and put tidily in the box they had brought for the purpose.

Ruth looked around to see what had happened to Annette. Her eye was caught by Cheryl, who was undoing the wing-nut at the top of her large cymbal. She saw Ruth looking her way and the nut fell in the grass.

"Damn!"

'Shall I help?' thought Ruth, 'or shall I just stand here and laugh at her?' Well there was really no lasting satisfaction to be had from sneering, so she knelt down on the grass beside the searching drummer and found the object straight away quite accidentally by putting her hand on it.

"Thanks," said Cheryl, carefully removing the cymbal and replacing the nut on the thread before giving it several turns. "We're playing at the Black Cat tonight," she added with assumed nonchalance. "Want to come and help with the backing, on rhythm guitar?"

"That rather depends, Cheryl."

"Depends?"

"On whether I get an apology for the hurtful things you said."

"Oh!"

Apologies did not come easily to Cheryl. She looked at the ground and kicked at a discarded plastic cup. "I'm sorry," she said at last. "But I have to point out that it wasn't very nice for me. Shouldn't you be giving me an apology? You led me on then dropped me like a ton of bricks after one call from Ricky Balfour."

"A ton of bricks is usually considered remarkable for the noise it makes when it falls, not for the speed with which it is dropped."

"Don't joke about it," Cheryl reproached her. "How would you have felt in my place?"

"I'd have felt upset too," Ruth admitted. "I was in a difficult position, but you were the one who suffered for it. I'm very very sorry. Do you forgive me?"

"A bit."

"It has to be total, Cheryl."

"I haven't stopped hurting yet."

"Neither have I. But don't worry. I promise I won't lead you on again."

"Oh," said Cheryl in a disappointed voice. "Is that supposed to be a favour?"

"Yes. Well it's the right thing to do, isn't it?"

"Or in this case not to do?"

"Not to do the wrong thing is a way of doing the right thing because..." Ruth glanced around in embarrassment... "Look, sweetheart, I hadn't expected to have to argue about it. Certainly not in a public place where anybody..."

She broke off as Barney appeared and pushed past with the bass drum in his arms.

"Come on lazy-bones. Do some of the work!" he called to his sister.

Cheryl picked up the box containing maracas and other hand-held percussion. She balanced the double bongos on the top of it.

"Will you come?" she asked again as she passed Ruth on her way to the van.

"I might. But I warn you I haven't got the confidence I used to have before... before... I was... attacked."

She still could not say the word 'raped'.

"Time to start on the long road back, then, isn't it?"

"You're priceless. You know that?"

"Want me to pick you up? Then you won't have to go home alone in the dark."

"Yes please."

They smiled at one another. Cheryl walked off jauntily with her arms full of the accoutrements of her trade and Ruth watched her go, wishing she could always feel this happy. But she had come to realise that it was a foolish happiness, one that she could not pursue. She must cherish this glimpse of it while it was there, like a shaft of sunshine in January.

"Are you not speaking to me anymore?" Ruth turned to find Annette at her side, trumpet case in hand. "I know I messed up on my top C, but it isn't a hanging offense."

"It ought to be," said Ruth. "But I didn't notice," she lied. "And to prove it, let me buy you something long and cool."

"I'd love an ice cream."

"So would I."

They walked together across grass which was brown and beaten down from the ministrations of many feet, littered with bottle tops, sweet papers, unsuccessful tombola tickets and candy-floss sticks.

"Harold bought me a lemonade earlier." Ruth informed her.

"He knows," said Annette.

"You told him?"

"I had to. He could tell something was up."

"What did he say?"

"I guess I'd forgotten what a smooth operator he can be. That's why he's so good at business, I suppose."

"So what did he say?"

They arrived at the ice-cream unit.

"I'll have a raspberry ripple," said Annette.

Ruth paid for two ice-creams and as soon as they turned away, they were besieged by the Mackenzie children, homing in on the goodies. Ruth would have ground her teeth, had it been safe to do so. But instead she bought three more ices, while Annette gave her needy sons some small change to spend on the depleted side shows. Harold could be glimpsed in the beer tent, chatting to some business friend he had chanced upon. It would not be long before he came to reclaim his wife.

"So tell me quick, before I die of curiosity."

"He said that if this guy thought anything of me at all," Annette told her between licks, "he wouldn't expect me to go flying off to live among strangers. (Lick Lick.) He would come here and talk it over with my husband, man to man. (Lick Lick.) I must be out of my mind, he said. It was a recipe for disaster, he said. Whoops! I've dropped some on my shoe."

"So what did you say?"

"I said he was right. I was out of my mind. But this wasn't a case of the mind. It was a case of the heart. Then of course he said that you can't live according to your emotions. (Lick Lick.) Emotions come and go, he said, and were apt to leave you high and dry. (Lick, Slurp.) And of course he's right, Ruth. He's always right." She bit the end off her cone. "I hate him."

"So what are you going to do?"

"I've written, but I haven't posted it. It would hurt him. It would hurt me too. My children would never forgive me."

"I'd like to say I hope it works out for you, but the trouble is I'm prejudiced. I don't want you to go."

"Even now you've got Cheryl?"

Ruth shot her a sideways look.

"Nobody's 'got' Cheryl. And if I had she couldn't replace you."

"I saw your face as she walked away," Annette observed. "Don't lay your dreams under her feet, will you."

"And what about you? Where are you going to lay your dreams?"

Annette glanced at the beer tent and turned her back on it quickly. But Harold had seen the gesture. He quickly finished his conversation and strode across the grass to reclaim his wife.

14

Raggle Taggle had set up their equipment in the long room at the back of the Black Cat which was used for wedding receptions and such-like functions. They had tuned in and ordered the drinks, which they liked to keep sip-ready on any flat surface that presented itself – the well-stained top of the amplifier, for instance. Playing was thirsty work.

It was that stage of the evening when practically nothing was happening and almost nobody was there yet; the 'dead dance hall' hour, which sensible musicians would take advantage of to warm up and try out new pieces they were unsure of, or even those which they enjoyed playing but which were not popular with the public.

After Ruth had plugged in her guitar and tuned it in a corner, Barney introduced her over the microphone as a guest star from the smash hit group the Stonemasons. This brought forth a spattering of applause from the few early-comers.

Hoping to please her, the boys asked her if they might try *The Cat That Walks Alone* and would she like to sing the vocals? She agreed to 'give it a go', since it was their venue not hers, so it was no loss to her if it caused their stock to fall and they were never asked to play there again.

Fortunately they made a reasonable job of coming in with the right vocal responses at the right time. They must have gone to the trouble of learning their part of the lyrics by heart. Afterwards she turned to the audience and put out a hand towards her fellow musicians as a signal to the gathering to give her colleagues a round of applause. The clapping was thin, but quite sincere and gladly accepted.

Then as the audience grew in number, Raggle Taggle ran through its usual repertoire of songs made popular by other groups. Gradually the number of people grew and things began to warm up until, by the interval, there was quite a lively crowd enjoying itself.

Raggle Taggle imbibed so much liquor that the second half seemed to flash by in a foggy trice. Cheryl stuck to cordials because she was the van driver, but Ruth had taken more alcohol than was her habit, in an effort to calm her nerves. She had stayed in the background as much as she could. It was difficult for her to feel at ease in this environment. She became shaky whenever she saw a cluster of youths together, which of course was quite often, since it was a Saturday night. She would have been scared of going home alone.

Bar closing time, the signal for customers to drink up and leave, arrived as they reached the end of their repertoire; after which they unplugged their equipment and began to stack it back in the van, so as to have it available to rehearse with during the week.

"Want a drink?" Barney asked Ruth. He had bought some bottles while the bar was still open.

"No thanks," said Ruth. She was still feeling the effects of her over-consumption during the interval. Not only that, but the house-hunting, the supervising of small children at the fete, the confrontation with Cheryl and an evening of playing to the public were a series of activities she was not really ready for all in one day. She shouldered her guitar wearily.

"Want to go home?" Cheryl asked her, noticing how washed-out she looked.

"Yes please, if you don't mind."

So they carried their last bits and pieces to the van without stopping to imbibe.

"Tell the old fogies I'll be home later, if they ask," Cheryl called to her brother.

"This is later," Barney replied.

"Then tell them not to wait up."

"How will Barney get home?" Ruth asked once they were in the van.

"They can walk. There's three of them. They've put all their gear in the van. They've got nothing to carry."

She started the engine and turned out onto the main road for Chorley.

It was late. A harvest moon glowed like a giant nectarine in the dark south-eastern sky. Autumn was already putting out flyers for its impending arrival with a litter of multi-coloured leaves on the pavements. They came floating down from sycamore, ash and oak and landed on the bonnet and the windscreen, only to fly off and pile up in the gutters, where a few yellow ochre lime leaves and scarlet ones from flowering cherry enriched the mix.

"When are you going to get yourself a better flat?" Cheryl wanted to know as they took the road towards Adlington. "Want me to help you find a place?"

"Not any more," said Ruth. "Can you take that turning there?"

"Which turning?"

"There on the right. We're just coming to it... there... wait for that car! Now! Turn here."

Cheryl did as she was told and without mishap entered the narrow lane which led up the hill into Anderton.

146

"Pull into the side here." Ruth ordered, when they had gone some way up the hill. "Into this gateway. That's the one."

"Are you feeling car sick again?"

"No no. There's something I want you to see. It'll answer your question."

There were no lamp posts in the lane. The only lighting came from the yellowy moon.

"See that farmhouse across the field?" asked Ruth. "That's going to be my home."

The building was black and slightly reddish-amber in the unusual light. The walls seemed eyeless with their missing window panes. Crooked trees grabbed at each other with long black-fingered branches.

"Are you serious?" squeaked Cheryl. "It looks like something from a horror movie."

"Only because it's dark," snapped Ruth. Cheryl was right. It did look like the set for a night of ghosts and vampires. But why did she have to say so and spoil the moment?

"I'll show it to you in the daylight some time, when you can get a better idea of its possibilities. You can drive on now."

But Cheryl switched off the engine and the headlights.

"I said you can drive on," repeated Ruth nervously.

"Not yet," said Cheryl. She switched on the interior light over the windscreen. She was feeling somewhat snubbed in that Ruth had showed no desire to take advantage of the fact that they were alone together in the dark. She opened the glove compartment and brought out a thermos flask and two cups in readiness for plan B.

Ruth watched her, wondering what was coming.

"I'm very tired," she pleaded.

Cheryl clicked her tongue in exasperation. She poured some coffee into one of the mugs , added a drop of whiskey, and handed it to Ruth.

"Drink that," she said. "It's guaranteed to revive."

"What is it?"

"My secret potion. What does it smell like?"

"Irish coffee."

"That's what it is. No drugs. It's to keep us both awake. Now you can tell me about Sarah,"

"Sarah? Who's been talking to you about Sarah?"

"Nobody's been talking to me. I overheard part of a conversation between Eileen and Lucy at the fete, after you'd gone. Eileen said something to the effect of, 'at least she hasn't tried to do away with herself again, like she did when Sarah left.' They were talking about you. So. Who's Sarah?"

"Can't we talk at my flat?" pleaded Ruth.

"That hell-hole? It's much more pleasant here." Cheryl sipped her coffee and settled back comfortably in her padded seat. "Anyway, you could always order me out at the flat. I'm the boss here. So come on, who's Sarah?"

"She was a friend of mine. A close friend. Too close, as it turned out."

"In what way was it too close?

"It's a long story, Cheryl, and it's very late."

"That's why I asked while we were here. It's too spooky out there for you to climb out and run away. You're my prisoner."

"How can you be so cruel?"

"Maybe I've learned it from you. So spill the beans. I want to know, Andy. I want you to tell me about Sarah. How did you meet?"

"I was in my final year at Music College. I was leading a perfectly normal student life. I worked hard and I played hard. I even had a boyfriend, a cellist called Robin. He was nice, but we were not serious. It was just somebody to go out to hops and concerts with."

"Sounds fun."

"It was. We all enjoyed our time as students. But, like most of the others, I was often short of money. So I used to make a little extra by standing in with a jazz band in the city."

"Playing piano?"

"No. Trumpet. Nev played piano. He was the band-leader. Sarah was the vocalist. She wasn't a student, she was married to Nev."

"They were older than you?"

"Nev was about thirty, which seemed ancient to me then, as it must to you now."

Cheryl gave a short laugh, because indeed it did.

"I was just twenty-two," Ruth continued. "Sarah was four years older. She and Nev had two children. Their little boy was only six months old when I first knew them, and the little girl was not quite three, so Sarah was very much tied at home during the day. She had very little social life.

"Nev was a good jazz pianist, but a difficult character to be around. I felt I had to tread carefully with him, if you know what I mean. He had that animal magnetism that can draw admirers. He could turn on the charm and make himself very attractive. But he could be quite malicious if you trod on his feet, as it were.

"I could see that he and Sarah were not happy together. He used to speak to her sarcastically a lot of the time. He'd often leave her alone and go off with the other guys, or other women if the opportunity presented itself."

"Did he make a pass at you?"

"Oh yes."

"What happened?"

"I gave him the brush-off, of course. Which didn't go down very well. After that Sarah and I used to be left to ourselves, while the fellers went off for their drinks or to do whatever fellers do between sets. Then she would talk to me.

She had had to move away from her family and friends when she married so she spent her days alone with the children. She invited me round for morning coffee once or twice. I gave her what time I could spare. Too much, perhaps. But she was very unhappy and she needed someone to talk to. Talking came very easily between us. We spoke the same language. She always understood what I was saying before I finished saying it and I always knew what she was feeling without her telling me. I was drawn to her, I decided, because I wanted to help her. That's what I said to myself. But looking back I can see quite clearly that I wanted her from the moment we met. It wasn't the first time I'd been attracted to another girl, of course. Lots of us got crushes at school. But the staff were always on the look-out and dealt pretty firmly with any friendship that was getting too intense."

"It was the same at mine. Instant separation."

"Or close supervision. And I came to a point where I had to admit to myself that my feelings for Sarah were something the school staff would have put the dampers on. However, she needed me so much I couldn't walk away. Maybe I couldn't have walked away even if her need hadn't been so great. Maybe I needed her too. But why speculate? It's all water under the bridge now."

"So tell me about this water that flowed under the bridge."

Ruth clutched her mug with both hands and stared at the grim house across the field as the swollen moon traversed the tree-tops overhead.

"When Nev realised that his wife had found someone to confide in," she continued, "he didn't seem to like it at all. He started finding ways to make us look foolish in each other's eyes, or making anti-feminine remarks in the hope of picking a fight with me. This lasted until Christmas, and the next term he was just as bad again by Easter."

"What about your final exams?"

"Oh I was still studying and practising, and playing jazz too."

"You didn't leave the jazz group?" Cheryl sounded surprised.

"No, Cheryl. So help me I didn't. Not until it was too late."

"How was that?"

"One evening he got drunker than usual and kept deliberately changing key while Sarah was singing. For a joke, I think, because he was giggling like an idiot while he did it. The bass and the guitar tried to keep with him, but gave up, so there was just him and Sarah. He started swearing at her for losing pitch. He made her look a total fool in front of everybody. She rushed out of the room crying.

"I started to follow her but he announced that we were going to play one of my solo numbers... I think it was 'Livery Stable Blues'. One that depends on the trumpet, anyway, and he sent the trombonist to haul me back."

"So did Nev do the same to you?"

"He tried, but I managed to keep up with him. The guys on clarinet and trombone gave up and that left only me and him and the drummer, who didn't have to keep switching into key after key, for obvious reasons. You can't imagine what it sounded like."

"But didn't the audience notice?"

"Of course they did. And so did the manager. He came along and asked Nev what the hell he was playing at. So Nev told him that it was this silly woman playing games. He said that I was trying to show off and he was doing his best to follow me. So the manager told me I was a liability. He gave me a couple of quid and said to pack up my trumpet and get out."

"And did you?"

"Of course. I had to. He was the boss."

"And nobody came to your support?"

"If you knew Nevil you wouldn't ask that question. He never failed to take revenge at the slightest hint of criticism. And his revenges could be very nasty."

"What about Sarah? Wasn't she there?"

"Sarah came back into the room as I was leaving it. I gave a helpless sort of shrug. She looked at Nev, then back at me without speaking. Before either of us could say anything Nev took her arm and led her up to the microphone, where he announced her next song." Ruth bit her lip at the memory. "It was one he had written himself, but it hadn't been played very often, because some of the audience had complained that it wasn't very nice."

"How do you mean? Was it obscene?"

"It was very anti-feminine."

"Sort of – 'Ya boo sucks to you, ha ha' kind of song?"

"That's not a bad description. It was called 'Oh Silly Woman'" Ruth swallowed and sipped her drink. Cheryl waited in a sympathetic silence.

"He sat at the piano," continued Ruth, "and played the introduction and they all started up. It was a vocal number, of course, which meant that Sarah sang the words

"But surely she wouldn't—"

"I'm afraid she did. I could either make a scene or go. So I went. The last thing I heard as I left was Sarah singing 'Oh silly woman, what a mess you're in. No-one to love and sozzled with gin – Need I go on?"

"No thanks. I've heard enough."

"Now do you understand why they were afraid to stand up to him?"

"How did you feel?"

"I felt sort of scalded. I can't describe it better than that. I had to ignore my feelings, though. My exams were about to begin and I needed to give them my undivided attention. But all that night Sarah's face haunted me. Oh Silly Woman, she sang and Oh Silly Woman echoed through my head all night. There was only one thing to do. It was what I should have been doing all that time."

"Practicing for your exams, I hope."

"Yes, and I found them such a welcome escape that I wished I had never neglected them. After a couple of days I felt fit and ready to concentrate on giving them my full attention."

"Let's face it, Andy, they were much more important than…"

"… than all that jazz. Yes I know that now. I knew it then. I thought Sarah was out of my life. I was determined not to give her another thought. She was somebody's wife. She didn't belong to me. She belonged to Nev. That didn't lessen the pain of course."

"Surely you could see you were well rid of them."

"Oh I could," Ruth conceded. "It would have been far better for me if that had been the end of the affair right there. In fact, I actually decided that I would never see either of them again."

"So what happened?"

15

"One evening, just before my finals, I was swotting up on the origins of the classical symphony – Haydn and all that – when out of the blue Sarah turned up at my digs with little Mandy and baby Theolonius, who was about one by then."

"Theolonius?"

"That's what the poor little lad was called. After Theolonius Monk, the jazz pianist, presumably."

"A bit unkind to the child, though."

"The least of Nev's unkindnesses, I'd say. Sarah seemed to be scared out of her wits. She begged me to hide them, so I let them stay the night. The three of them slept in my bed while I lay on the eiderdown on the floor. But I couldn't keep them there, of course. So next day we scraped together enough money between us for the train fare and I took them south to my Grandfather. His house is big enough to sleep a whole orchestra!"

"What!"

"Well, the string section, anyway."

"There's a lot of musicians in a string section."

"Exactly, and, most importantly, it was a place Nev didn't know the existence of. There's plenty of garden there for children to play in and no close neighbours. Grannie and Grandad had lost both their sons in the First World War. My mother was the only one left of their children, and she married late because fit and eligible men were hard to find in her young day. Well, she eventually became a clergyman's wife, which meant that her married life was spent in various church residences, often some distance from Grannie and Grandad. The old folk didn't see us as often as they would have liked. We used to go there for visits, but not to live. So Fettleford Hall, or Fettles, as we called it..."

"To rhyme with nettles?"

"Well there were plenty of them there, believe me. Anyway, Fettles had never actually been my home. The old people hadn't had any younger generation to keep them lively in their declining years. It was a very sad house.

"When I brought Sarah to them, her children were soon running around the place, bringing back childish voices and laughter. It gave the old folk a new lease of life. Grannie looked after us and Grandfather found Sarah some paid work in the office on the estate, while I went back to college. But I'd missed most of the written exams and never stood a chance of getting any qualifications."

"Oh no!"

"Yes. I regretted it at the time; and more so since. But I was absolutely besotted with Sarah by then. She was like half of me. We were happy together like happy is supposed to be. It's hard to say 'no' to happiness, Cheryl."

"Hard, but sometimes you have to."

"Happiness is life-enhancing. It makes you realise what a great place Heaven must be... worth making the effort to get there. It's when it's taken from you that your life falls apart. But I know now what I didn't know then, when I took that overdose..."

"You took an overdose!"

"That's what Eileen and Lucy were talking about. If it hadn't been for Lucy, you and I would not be sitting here now."

"I had no idea..."

155

"And I'm so grateful that they saved me, because I know now that you can recover and the experience will leave you stronger, if you let it. Then a certain talented girl drummer came along and I found happiness again."

Cheryl took her hand and kissed it.

"Nothing is forever in this life, is it," she said, "bad or good."

"Exactly. But at that time I thought me and Sarah were forever. So I went back to join her at my grandparents' place and found what employment I could in the area. I got the organist's job at the local church. I gave music lessons."

"You should have been doing better things than that."

"I know, but life doesn't always deal you the cards you want. And anyway, I was happy. The grandparents were happy. Sarah said it was the happiest time of her life. The children loved it there.

"She'd registered them with the local health authority, of course, so that they could have access to the local clinic and be put on the register for the doctor and the dentist and she could receive her family allowance. Then when Mandy turned five she started attending the local infants' school." Ruth paused and drained her mug. "I think that must have been how Nev found out where we were."

"Through the official channels?"

"Unknown to us, he'd hired a private detective. We'd had no hint of trouble, until one morning Nev turned up at the Fettles with two law enforcement officers. They bundled little Theo howling into their car then went to pick up Mandy from her school. Sarah was never able even to say goodbye to her. It wasn't until the next day that she had a letter from Nev's lawyer to say that the children had been made wards of court and Sarah was forbidden contact with them."

"He couldn't do that, surely!"

"Well he did. Sarah was distraught. She went to the authorities and they suggested that she start legal proceedings to try and get her children back. When she was granted some access under supervision, we moved back North to be close to them. We rented a house in Chorley, which was close enough without being too close.

"But it was hard for her, only to see them in a formal setting and not have them around her like a proper mum. The closeness was gone. After every meeting with them she would return deeply upset. And I was helpless to take away her pain."

Ruth paused. Cheryl took the empty cup from her hands, filled it with even more strongly fortified coffee and replaced it into the still-cupped hands.

"I used to hear her crying in the night," continued Ruth. "One night she crawled into my bed, sobbing. I put my arms around her, to comfort her."

She lifted the brandified cup to her face and drank.

"And?"

"We became lovers."

"Not till then?"

"Not till then. Never while the children were with us. I didn't know it was going to happen. I hadn't known what it could be like."

"And what was it like?"

"Addictive, my love. That's what makes it dangerous. And from that time on we slept there together every night. It was a mistake, of course, because it gave Nevil exactly what he was looking for. When the hearing eventually took place they decided not to release the children into the care of adults who were in an unnatural relationship."

"But they couldn't have known you were sleeping together."

"The detective took photographs. None of the pictures was conclusive in itself. But there was a photo of us walking along one of the paths holding hands and there was one shot of us greeting one another with a kiss on the doorstep. He even got a shot of us asleep together in the same bed. So I was told. I

157

never got to see them because Sarah's lawyer told me she would stand a better chance if I stayed away." Ruth drained her coffee, shook out the drops out of the window and put the cup on the dashboard. "As if it made any difference!" she continued. "In the end it was Sarah's word against that of the wronged husband. And the photographs were regarded as sufficiently damning to be taken seriously."

"But how could he have possibly photographed you in bed together?" protested Cheryl, sipping at her own emptying cup. "What did he do? Hide in a loft or something?"

"I don't know. Maybe he got a ladder and took it to our window. We never bothered about drawing the curtains. There were no other houses nearby."

"You must have felt pretty sick when you found out what he'd done."

Everything about that time was sickening," sighed Ruth. "Sarah had had to endure that long wait while the legal proceedings were pending. All that time she only saw her children under supervision and for short periods. Also during this time both my grandparents died. They had been part of our happiness and they too had been taken away."

"What about the house? Who looks after it now?"

"My parents live in Fettles now that my father's retired. I don't often go there because it makes me sad. Those two lovely people, who had taken us under their wing and made us all so happy; they're not there any more and without them it feels desolate."

"But why would Sarah leave you? When she'd lost her children anyway? Didn't she need you all the more?"

"That wasn't the end."

"Oh?"

Ruth did not want to go on. This was going to be the hardest part to speak about. She had never spoken about it to anybody. She thought she never would. But Cheryl was waiting. Cheryl was employing an unaccustomed spur of silence. Ruth decided to get it over with and speak the unspeakable.

"Once Nev had won custody of the children," she began, "he became very kind and considerate to Sarah. He became the charming, reasonable, attractive man that Sarah had known when she became his wife. He told her she could come and see the children whenever she wanted to, if she came alone."

Ruth sank back in her seat and laid her head against the back-rest.

"If she came alone," repeated Cheryl.

"Exactly. Do I need to go on?"

"Yes," said Cheryl, taking Ruth's hand and kissing it again. "You do need to."

'She's right', Ruth acknowledged to herself. 'I must get it all out'. It hurt her to go over the painful past, but she had carried the wound in silence for too long. Now she was letting out the poison and already she was beginning to feel a slight easing of the pain.

"So off Sarah went," she continued. "She didn't need to be asked twice. When she returned, I knew at a glance what had happened. She was rosy with pleasure and she could not look me in the eye."

"No need to spell out what had gone on, then."

"Of course they were husband and wife, so they were entitled to do whatever they liked together. But she made no attempt to spare my feelings. She was oozing self-satisfaction. It was almost as though I wasn't there. I can't tell you how... how... sidelined... that made me feel."

"Betrayed would be a better word."

"Anyway she eventually sat me down, poured me a stiff whisky and told me that Nev had offered to take her back on the condition that she gave up all contact with me. She told me that she didn't want to leave me, but she had to go back to Nev for the sake of the children.

"But… but… she'd ruined your future! How could she just walk out on you?"

"When you have children there's only one choice, she said. Children come first, she said."

"Isn't that what parents tend to say whenever they want to use their children as an excuse to get out of something?"

"Maybe, but children do come first. Everybody says so. Isn't that what they say? Annette says children come first. So does Lucy."

"Yes," agreed Cheryl. "But it doesn't mean the parents haven't got to consider anybody else at all. Especially when it involves obligations to other people. If friends have made the kind of sacrifices that you did, they're owed a bit more than just 'Cheerio'."

"Not if it means…"

"If you look at Annette and Lucy, you have to see that they've got very busy lives outside of their families. Their children grow up and have lives of their own. Friends may still be there when the children have left home. Friends deserve some loyalty, don't they?"

"Of course they do. Otherwise I would never have answered Ricky's call for help. You know – that time when I wanted you so badly and I was just about to prove it when the phone went."

"You wanted me so badly?" Cheryl felt she had been somehow wrong-footed. "Did you really want me so badly?" "That's not how it seemed to me."

"I know. And I'm sorry. And I wish you could forgive me."

"There is a way."

Ruth sighed.

"Is that what you want?"

"Not if you don't. I'm not begging for it. But you keep messing me about."

"Do I? Is that how you saw it? I was thinking of you."

"Thinking of me? Thinking of *me*? Don't lie."

"I hadn't stopped to consider, when we almost finished up in bed, what it might do to you. But now I have. Honestly, sweetheart, it's better not to go down that road."

"Shouldn't I have some say in the matter?"

"No."

"Well I think I should have," insisted Cheryl, who was a complete stranger to not having a say.

"And there's something else," Ruth continued, ignoring Cheryl's indignation. "Something I haven't told you. In fact I haven't told anybody."

"I'm not sure I want to hear it."

"It's something you ought to know."

Cheryl said nothing.

"I'm pregnant," said Ruth.

There was a long silence. The moon found a cloud to hide behind, and the night was suddenly darker. Inside the van everything was completely still.

"Say something," pleaded Ruth. "Talk to me."

"Is it – Ricky's?"

"Goodness, no. He's not interested in me that way. Nor I in him. That's why we like one another. We know where we are with each other. No expectations. No complications."

"You can't mean it's from the rape!"

"Well there's no other way I could be pregnant. But that is what I am, apparently. Pregnant. Sweet are the uses of adversity."

Cheryl gathered up the cups and rattled about, bundling them back into the glove compartment before blurting out;

"But you can't keep it! There must still be enough time left to come to your senses and get rid of it."

"I'm not getting rid of it. I want to keep it."

"But you don't know what it… you don't know who it's part of."

"It's a part of me. That's what matters. I hug it to myself, like

161

a little nugget of gold. Infinitely precious. Bringing up a child is a privilege, so Lucy told me. It doesn't matter where it comes from or how it is conceived. That's what she said."

"Yes but is she right?"

"I don't know," said Ruth. "But I want to find out."

In icy silence Cheryl started up the van and switched on the headlights. She did a five-point turn in the gateway and drove back down the hill onto the main road.

'I've offended her again,' thought Ruth. 'She gets offended much too easily. But maybe it's better this way. It won't be so hard for me to stick to my friendship-only decision.'

"So you do understand why I didn't make love to you just now when I had the opportunity?" Ruth voiced her concern to the silent presence by her side. "It's not that I wasn't tempted. It's because I made a resolution not to. Because I don't want what happened to me to happen to you."

"Hah!" snorted Cheryl. "Why should it? I'm not you. And you're not Sarah."

"No-o but… "

"You don't have to make excuses. You could at least have kissed me. There's nothing wrong with that. It isn't wicked to kiss, even if it's another girl."

"Ye-es, but" Ruth was not made of stone. She knew better than Cheryl did what that kiss would lead to. "I did try to kiss you once before," she pointed out, "only it foundered on the rocks of that horrible sofa and my fear for my broken face."

"You could have tried again. It wouldn't have 'foundered', as you so quaintly put it, in this cosy van. Nor would I have got rough on your delicate little mouth.

"Ye-es, but…"

"'Yes but' means nothing to me," snapped Cheryl. She put her foot down and they zoomed down the lane to the Chorley Road much faster than was advisable.

An uneasy silence hung about them while the van sped on over a stretch of gently undulating tarmac.

Cheryl sat grimly clutching the steering wheel.

'I've given her all my sympathy,' she was thinking, 'I've listened to her and supported her all the way. All right, so she's been treated badly, but she has no consideration for other people's feelings. She doesn't care how I feel. Why have I wasted so much time on her?'

They were coming into the centre of Chorley and had slowed down and stopped at the behest of a set of traffic lights on red, when Cheryl remembered why she had spent so much time with Ruth.

"This baby you insist upon having," she came out with anxiously, "It won't prevent you from joining my new group, will it?"

There was no reply, because by this time Ruth was asleep.

Cheryl put out a hand and shook her companion's shoulder mercilessly while she repeated the question more loudly.

"And please don't tell me I'm priceless," she added, when Ruth opened her eyes.

"Oh Cheryl," sighed Ruth wearily. "It's a great big man's world out there. Do you really think there's room in it for a bunch of silly women?"

"I don't know," replied Cheryl, "but I want to find out."

The lights turned green. The van moved on.